PROTECTING HER

THOMPSON BROTHERS
BOOK THREE

SUMMER COOPER

LOVY BOOKS

EMBER

Ember

London, United Kingdom

My fingers strummed the strings of the guitar as they moved easily from one chord to the next in the song. I forgot about the frigid cold that made my fingers ache, the far too familiar pang of hunger in my belly, and the way passers-by either grumbled about beggars on the street or flung coins into the guitar case. I'd also forgotten the way the knit wool cap over my hair made my head itch. In that moment, I was lost in my song and the memories it evoked for me.

That was why I didn't notice the man at first. My mind was in the past, in a time when my grandmother's guitar was all that gave me peace. Whether my parents were zoned out on their drug of choice, or hyper and frenetic as the drugs made them manic, that old guitar was what kept me calm and unafraid. Some nights, I'd go to bed hungry because I hadn't been able to steal any money from my mom so I could buy food. Some nights she would bring food home, and I'd ferret things away to eat once her mood switched and she forgot about me again. Other nights, I'd go to bed afraid of the sounds I could hear outside of my room, of the shouts and screams that could be laughter or anger. I never knew which and hid under my covers so I didn't have to find out.

Gran had taken care of me from the time I was born until she died when I was six-years-old. I'd managed to hang onto the guitar, though Mom had sold all of Gran's other possessions, as if she hadn't cared about her mother at all. When Mom had reached for it, I'd run to the guitar, clutched it to my chest, and glared at my mother with hatred in my eyes until she looked away and moved on. The guitar had been by my side ever since. I'd even had a locker at the bus station I'd put it in when I knew Mom was really hard up for cash, just to make sure she didn't sell it.

I'd also learned to hang out in the park until the very last light of day. Little girls with curly blonde hair and round brown eyes could be a target to some of the men who came home with my mother, and I'd learned a long time ago how to avoid them. Stay in the park, go straight to my room and find my stash of food, and shove my dresser in front of my door. It had kept me safe so far.

It had been this old guitar that had drawn Graham to

me. He'd been nineteen my senior year of high school, and he'd completely swept me off of my feet. He'd approached me in the park I used to hang out in and asked me about the guitar, as if he knew I was a sucker for that guitar. I hadn't protested when he'd asked me to play it, but I hadn't been too sure about my ability to do the guitar justice, even if those sweet blue eyes of his had told me I could. I'd been nervous to play for an audience, but my fingers soon stopped slipping off the wrong chords, and I'd begun to sing.

I thought I'd captivated him with my voice and guitar the way he'd captured me with a sardonic smile. That smile had said he'd known I could play and he'd never doubted me. I thought he'd fallen in love with me then that the world had forever changed for us. Turns out, he just saw a way to panhandle without doing any work himself.

Oh, not right away. Graham had given me time to graduate, or to at least finish my last classes, before he'd swept me away to a new life. He'd even left me, ahem, untouched, until we made it to his hometown in Kentucky. We'd panhandled our way up to the small coal town, well, I had, and we'd arrived in the middle of the night. His friends had found him, us, a house there, and he'd waited until he had me totally alone, totally of legal age, before he'd laid a finger on me. There'd been kisses and promises of passion before that, but he'd always waited, and that had made me love him more.

For a moment, a scent intruded into my reverie, and I looked up to see a rather handsome man sat on a bench across from me. I noted his interest, but the song caught me again, and I was in the past. Graham had gone out with his friends a lot, but he always came home with lots of money. He was a poker player, and if he'd had a good night, he'd tell me. I let it go, because I was too stupid, too naïve, to think otherwise about the man I loved.

I could deal with the fact that he wasn't a great lover, though he wasn't bad. I wasn't naïve enough to not know what good sex was supposed to be; I'd seen movies, and I had read avidly. Graham always seemed to finish just as things really started to get good for me, but I didn't complain. Sex wasn't everything, and he always made sure I was warm, comfortable, and fed. He'd called me his little woman, and it made me proud.

He needed me, he needed me to cook, clean, and to love him. Graham was an orphan, and he'd never known a real home. I gave him that, and in return, he made sure I had what I wanted. So what if he earned his money through poker? It was better than working down in a mine or at a factory. I had to admit now, I let a lot pass me by.

One day, Graham came with a new plan. Sometimes he had some of these off the wall ideas, and I'd learned they rarely went far, so I didn't pay much attention to this plan. He wanted to take me to England, a place I'd always wanted to visit, and get me into the music industry there. He'd show me castles and manor houses during the days, and in the evenings, I'd play music in pubs and other places in these giant cities.

"Oh, they love Americans there, Bridget, you'll be a star," he'd said as I stared at the application for a passport he'd brought to me. "We will have to change your stage name though."

"I thought I might." I'd stared glumly at the papers, at the name printed there. Bridget Jones. I'd always caught a lot of flak over that name. My mother had thought it was hilarious and had always told people she'd named me after the movie. I never kept a diary, though I probably should have because of that movie.

"You can use my last name if you want?" he'd said tentatively. He knew I wanted to get married, we'd been together over two years, but he'd always shied away from the subject.

I glared at the papers with enough anger that flames should curl the edges. "No, I'll call myself Ember Jones. Embers is Mom's maiden name. I'll just use that."

"Oh, cool; yeah, that will work. Great." He was flippant now, happy that he'd dodged another bullet.

I wasn't about to start another argument with him then anyway. I'd learned quickly it got me nowhere and only made him act irrationally. I'd signed the papers, taken them in with the money he'd given me to have it all processed at the passport facility in the post office, and had quickly forgot about it all. By the time the passport actually arrived, I'd started to think maybe it was time to leave Graham and head back to Alabama.

His behavior became erratic, and I kept finding white powder on the sink in the bathroom. I had a drug addict for a mother; I knew what that white powder was. But Graham had led a hard life, and I wanted to be there for him when others weren't. I'd left all I knew behind for him, and I knew we could fix this.

From the day I first saw him when I was seventeen, on the verge of eighteen, I knew Graham was the one for me. I'd wanted nothing more than to run away from my mother, to a place where people didn't know I was her daughter, or that my mom slept with men for money sometimes, and where I wouldn't get pity or scorn because I'd have a good man at my side. Yeah, he could be cranky, and sometimes, he was a downright asshole, but I loved him, and he loved me. It was us against the world, and that was all I'd needed.

When he'd come home with expensive luggage and plane tickets one day, I'd nearly lost my mind. He'd made all my dreams come true, so far, and this was one I wouldn't admit I'd really wanted to happen. I hadn't let myself dream that he could really take me to England, but there was the proof.

I'd always wanted to go, my favorite television shows were all British, my favorite books took place in England, and I loved the history of the country. I'd wanted to see the place where my great-grandmother came from, and to enjoy the life I didn't think I could have. I'd put away my protests and turned a blind eye to so much because I'd wanted to go.

For five and a half months, it had gone well. I'd played in pubs, met other singers who taught me new ways to play, who had taught me old folk songs, and introduced me to so much more. I'd learned to get over the fact that the language was so different and that the food wasn't the same at all. Although, sometimes I would go to KFC just for something familiar. I'd made friends and wanted to stay, but I knew the time was almost up.

That was when Graham had changed the world for me all over again. He'd said we were out of money, and had wanted me to do something I refused to do. He'd bought some drugs and wanted me to sell them to the friends I'd made.

"How dare you?" I'd croaked out around a sob of heartbreak. I'd stared at him, the heartache a burn in my eyes, as I'd tried to figure out who this guy was. "You should know better, Graham."

"Yeah, so what? Your mom was a meth whore, who doesn't have a sob story? Take this and get rid of it, or you can get the fuck out, *Ember*." He'd emphasized my stage name as he shoved a plastic bag full of packets of cocaine into my hand. I'd dropped the bag as if it had burned my hand and backed away from him.

"I'm serious, Bridge, you either get rid of this for me or get the fuck out." He'd stared me down, disgust and hate in eyes that had turned colder than ice. I could only stare at him, again lost for words.

"No."

"No?"

"No, Graham... I..." I felt the thickness of tears in my throat as a sob cracked my voice, but he didn't let me finish.

"Then get out."

He'd picked up my guitar case, my coat that I'd stuffed

my cap and gloves in, and thrown my purse at me. "Go on, leave."

"But, Graham, I need my ticket to get home."

"Nah, find your own way home, honey. I ain't paying for that shit too. Bye now." He'd held the door open to the house we'd rented and waved at the empty air outside.

"Graham, you're not serious? It's freezing out there!" I'd protested, but he'd given me a look so hateful I knew he meant it. He'd come close to hitting me more than once. He'd punched the wall next to the side of my head or kicked over things so often in our early relationship—and more since he'd started to use drugs—that I knew what that look meant.

He was on the verge. And just like that, I'd become homeless, without funds, and in a whole lot of trouble. I had to be out of England within the next two weeks, and I didn't have a plane ticket. I didn't know where to turn, and I'd left my phone with Graham somehow. I was afraid to go back there; the hate in his eyes had been so clear I knew that wasn't a smart thing to do.

I'd cried myself to sleep in a dark alley that first night. I knew I had one friend I could go to, but they were out of town for the next two weeks. Embarrassment at how Graham had treated me, shame at my predicament, and a little bit of stupidity meant that I had nowhere to turn. I'd found an empty house to sleep in the next day, but I was so damn hungry and unbelievably cold. I'd found enough change in the bottom of my bag to pay for a bottle of water and to use a public toilet at the nearest train station, but that had been it. I'd ended up in a park and had started to play the guitar, just as a way to pass some time, to clear my head, and come up with a plan. When people started to throw money into the case, I was shocked.

There was now enough money in there to buy a hot meal, or a couple bottles of water and some dry food like chips and bread that would last longer. I looked up, the song at an end, to see the stranger who smelled so nice was still on the bench across from me. He was a businessman, obviously. At least, the tailored navy-blue suit, expensive leather shoes, and haircut that left his brown hair long on top and short in the back said so.

He had a neatly trimmed beard along his jaw, but not too long. It was the eyes that caught my attention though, those light green eyes that stared at me in a way that made it feel as if he was puzzled and wanted to figure me out.

"What are you staring at?" I barked out; my jaw shook now that I wasn't preoccupied with the song. He looked like the kind of guy who would have money, money that could buy me a whole meal. I wanted to bark at him to get me food, the knot of hunger in my stomach had long gone from a twinge to outright pain, and I'd barely slept. I wasn't at my friendliest.

2

EMBER

Ember

"Just you. That was incredible. Why are you out here in the cold, when you should be in a warm concert hall with a voice like that?"

I'd learned my lesson from Graham. Don't pay attention to men with beautiful eyes and sardonic smiles; they'll just break your heart.

"A man like you left me with no other choice." The words were out before I'd even realized I was about to speak, and my cheeks heated up.

It wasn't his fault Graham had turned out to be a Grade-A Douchebag, with the capital letters and all. It wasn't his fault I was basically squatting in an abandoned building in London, far from home, without anywhere to turn. In my youth, I'd learned to make do and fend for myself. But this was a whole new ballgame. I wasn't allowed to rely on charity here. I couldn't ask for welfare; that had been made abundantly clear when I'd read up about it online in the library I'd visited yesterday. I was here on the Visa Waiver program, so I had no recourse to aid here. I couldn't even call home and ask for help. I didn't even know if my mom was still alive or not, and there wasn't anyone else to call.

Graham had discouraged me from making friends outside of the circle of men he knew or their girlfriends. At the time, he was all I needed anyway. Now, I wish I had someone, anyone, I could have relied on. I was also afraid Graham would find me. He'd been so angry at me that I had a feeling if he saw me again it wouldn't go well.

"Miss…" That melodic voice, that kind of reminded me of the accent of old Hollywood movie stars from the black and white films my grandmother had loved, broke into my thoughts again.

"Oh, sorry." I wasn't sure why I'd apologized. A habit I'd picked up from the British, I supposed. Hunger, fatigue, and fear washed over me in a wave that made me sway, and I rested my head against my guitar until it passed.

"Are you alright, miss?" I couldn't decide if his accent was American or British, or somewhere in between. In the melting pot of London, I'd heard so many accents and voices over the past months, that sometimes I wasn't even sure I was listening to English anymore. I might have absorbed a language through osmosis and started to understand others when they spoke other languages.

I wanted to laugh at that, but I was too tired to do it. I'd just rest my head here for a minute. Then I'd feel better and could go back to that cold place that at least had a flimsy lock on the door of the room I'd slept in.

"Miss?" This time his voice came from the same level as my head, and I opened weary brown eyes to look at him.

"Yes?" The urge to bark at him to give me food had left me now, and I just wanted to sleep. In a nice, soft, warm bed, covered with a thick duvet, as my head sank into a thick down pillow. The British might have food that I found odd, I still didn't know what kind of dessert Spotted Dick was, but they knew how to make a bed. In fact, I might even eat some of that oddly named dessert right now, if it was offered. I'd seen it on more than one menu, but I couldn't get past the laughter long enough to order it.

"Do you need some help?" His voice came with the clean smell of mint, and I smiled sleepily. "You're American, aren't you? Why don't you let another lost American offer you dinner?"

"You don't sound very American," I said, my voice soft as I rested there, barely able to lift my head from the guitar case. I was so tired, so hungry, that I could barely move.

"Well, that's easily explained. Why don't you let me buy you dinner, and I'll explain it all?" He didn't touch me, but something about his presence, his voice, soothed me.

"I know men like you," I started, but couldn't finish. I did too. Tears stung my eyes, and my voice felt thick, but I couldn't afford to lose that little bit of moisture so I tried to suck it up. I could barely lift my head to dash the tears away, but I managed. "What do you want?"

"Well, no offense, chipmunk, but you're hardly in a

condition that would warrant lust." I heard laughter in his voice, and that made me raise my head.

"Fine, so I don't look like a beauty queen right now. You wouldn't either if you hadn't eaten in three days and had been chucked out on your rear." Again, with the oversharing. I wanted to die of mortification but didn't have the energy.

"Wait, you've been without food for three days?" He stood up, took my guitar, to which I protested, and put it away. "Come with me, we're going to feed you."

He took my guitar in one hand and my hand in the other, and off we went. He didn't torture me by asking what I wanted or passing by a dozen shops before he found something suitable. He took me into the first restaurant we came across. Luckily, it was one of the new buffet-style restaurants, and the smell of food made my knees weak.

The man took me to a table, sat me down, and was soon back with a plate filled with food. "I didn't know what you'd want, but everyone likes salad, right? And, if you're a real American, you love Ranch dressing, so I put some of that on it. Here's some bread."

A waiter came by to ask what drinks we wanted, and the man ordered two coffees and two colas for us. I was too busy eating to worry about drinks.

"My name is Kevin, by the way," he said with a soft chuckle after I'd eaten enough to swallow some of the cola.

"I'm Bridge, uh, Ember."

"Bridge Ember?" he asked, perfectly shaped dark eyebrows knotted at the bridge of his nose.

"No, Ember, my name is Ember," I said with a grateful

smile. I'd at least managed to clean my teeth in the bath-room at the train station. I didn't have a toothbrush, but some rough paper towels had done the trick. For now.

His green eyes lit up as he watched me eat, and I felt strange when he didn't join in the free-for-all I'd partaken in, but I didn't care. I had food and lots of it. I passed different stations and saw one that was lit up with light that spelled out American cuisine. I went over and found fried cheese sticks, hot dogs, with coleslaw and chili for condiments, hamburgers, pot roast, and several other dishes. I filled my pockets with cheese sticks and didn't care who saw me. I also didn't care if the oil from the sticks stained my coat or made me fat. It was something I could eat later. When the man was gone.

I made my way back to the man and sat down with a hot dog covered in coleslaw and chili. I was a glutton with that much food available and didn't care. It occurred to me the man might want something in return for this treat, but at that moment, I was still too hungry to worry about it much. I had gained a bit of weight since we came to England. I'd learned to drink a lot more beer here, but I could still outrun him if he tried to get pervy with me.

"What was that song you were singing? Is it one you wrote?" He didn't appear to be in a rush to get me back to a hotel room; rather, he looked as if he never wanted to leave the place, although he hadn't eaten a thing.

"It's a song I wrote for my grandmother." She'd had a wild heart that longed to be free, but she'd married young, been widowed young, and had tried her best to raise my mom alone.

"I love your voice. It's like a young Stevie Nicks, but you have your own sound. It's enchanting, really." I studied him shrewdly, looking for a tease or bullshit, but nothing pinged on my radar.

"Thanks." I glanced out the window when I saw a familiar red flash, but it was a woman's scarf, not Graham's red hat. My heart had thumped in my chest when I saw that flash of red, but now it calmed down. "Um, do you mind if I get something else?"

"No, it's all you can eat, and you are obviously hungry." He gave me a subtle wink, and I slid out of the booth I was in.

I went to the desserts, found some chocolate cake and put some on my plate. I saw some hot fudge sauce and went wild as I poured it over the cake. I just didn't care, I had been hungry for too long.

"Tell me about your problems, what's going on with you?" He waited until I'd slid the empty plate away from me to ask the question.

I'd inhaled the cake, and at some point, I might be embarrassed about the amount of food I'd eaten, but for now I just sighed happily. I felt warm, at last, and sleepy as the food stretched my stomach.

"Oh, I'm just the typical stupid woman. I let my boyfriend talk me into coming to a country I've never been to before, without money of my own, or a way to work because I don't have a visa, and I'm about to overstay my welcome. Oh, he kicked me out when I refused to deal drugs for him." It wasn't like I'd ever see this guy again, so I spilled it all out. "I don't have the money to get back home, or a home to go to once I get back to America. It's all a giant shit storm, really."

"Wow. Yeah. It is. I think I might have a solution though, if you're willing to listen?" Kevin sat back in his booth and looked at me with that steady green gaze of his. I wanted to squirm under that gaze because I knew he had a bullshit radar as good as mine.

"I don't have sex with strangers for food," I said immediately, just to get that out of the way.

"And none is expected," he said with a rueful laugh. His eyes raked over me, and I pulled my coat tighter because I still had on the clothes I'd worn three days ago. I might look clean, but I didn't feel it.

That wasn't what he meant though. He seemed to be a genuinely nice guy, and for now I'd buy the story he was selling. I was desperate. Not desperate enough to traffic myself, but desperate.

"Look, my family owns a hotel nearby. That's all. I might be able to get you some help there. Obviously, you can't work here, but you can take the room I have to offer. And some food. So you can take those cheese sticks out of your coat pocket."

My face flamed bright red, I could feel it, but I did as he'd said. I didn't even know he'd seen me do that. I was so embarrassed, but there was nothing else I could do. I mulled over his offer and decided that if he was really an altruistic soul, then I'd take him up on that offer. A couple days was better than nothing.

"What do you want for that?" I asked finally. I had to know, right?

"Nothing, Ember. Just a thank you." He looked like the kind of guy who didn't usually have to ask for one, but this was new to me. I'd learned in my youth that men could be dangerous creatures.

More recently, I'd learned they could be heartless too. Tears stung my eyes again, and I scrunched up my nose as I tried to fight the sting away. Here I was, in a foreign country, with no home, unless you counted that dark room with no light and no heat, depending on the kindness of a total stranger. A handsome one who obviously had money to burn, but still a stranger. A male one.

I studied him deeply. His eyes were amused, but there was a kindness there that I didn't think he could fake. There was also curiosity. I took a deep breath as I looked down at his hands. Soft, without many callouses, his hands were clean, the nails manicured, and skin had a slight tan, as if he played outdoor sports, rather than the afterglow of a tanning bed or a vacation. Holiday, as the English called it.

He didn't look like a rapist, but then, what did I think they were supposed to look like? Looks could be deceiving, and I knew it well. My head said to run, to just go back to the cold, dark room and try to figure out where the American embassy was. Maybe they could help me? I wasn't sure, but as I looked into Kevin's eyes, something told me I could be sure about him.

I took a deep breath and nodded my agreement. "Okay, I'll go."

I knew it might be my biggest mistake yet, but when I thought about that cold room, how I could barely sleep because I was afraid, even with that door locked, I wanted the room that Kevin offered. I wanted a night of peace and a shower. Oh, a shower would be heaven!

"Do you have a bag somewhere?" he asked as he handed a debit card to the waiter who came to the table and didn't even blink.

"I... No, all I have is what you see."

"Do you have your passport?" he asked, his brows knitted. He looked so concerned, so sweet, when he did that. My heart fluttered, but I told it to shut the fuck up. We were done with men.

"Yeah, that stays in my guitar case. I don't go anywhere without either one." I wasn't totally stupid, after all. I had that lifeline anyway.

"Good. Come on then, let's get you settled in for the night." He took my hand, picked up my case from under the table, and led me out. I wasn't sure if I was about to head into a nightmare or not.

Kevin's hand felt far too good around mine to be anything but a dream.

3

KEVIN

Kevin

We strode down the busy street, her hand in mine, her shoes a squeak on the damp pavement. I wasn't quite sure why I hadn't let her hand go yet, but knew it felt nice. Her fingers were long and slim, and her palms were just the right size for cupping around the neck of a guitar. I'd seen her in that park, on the way to a meeting, and had totally forgot my appointment.

The sound of her voice had drawn me in first. I'd followed the sound until I found her, on that bench with her guitar. I'd sat as she sang a song about broken wings and faded dreams and wondered who had hurt her so much. Was the song her own or had she heard it somewhere else? She had a country music sound with a rock and roll edge that I liked. It was only after I'd studied her for a moment that I noted the lines of hardship around her mouth and the signs of exhaustion on the delicate skin beneath her eyes. Those bruised eyes told me she was hungry, had barely slept recently, and I'd wondered if this music, if her moment in the park wasn't panhandling but an escape.

Something deep in my chest had twinged, and I'd waited for her to stop her song to speak to her. She'd given me a look I could only describe as feral before she'd barked at me. Then, as if she'd lost control, she'd turned an attractive shade of pink and had backed off. When she'd regained control, she answered my questions.

I was surprised to hear an American accent, a Southern one at that, but shouldn't have been. My fellow Americans came here often. I explained my transatlantic accent to her then, how I'd been sent over here to boarding school, and that I'd spent most of my life here. I'd even gone to university here. I didn't exactly want to disclose that I'd gone to the poshest, most exclusive boarding school in the country, but not because she was poor.

No, the girl whom had sat across from me inhaling food wasn't the kind who would be impressed with names or prestigious schools, if she even knew what those schools were. From the frank way she spoke, I knew she was down to earth, and from the guarded look in her eyes, I knew she'd been hurt and hurt badly. I wasn't surprised when she revealed her story to me.

I wanted to find this Graham fellow and pound him into dust, but something about the way she talked about him spoke of fear. And if he was mixed up with drug runners here, well, it was bad news I'd walk into if it meant keeping her out of it; otherwise, I didn't want to get mixed up in any of that. Besides, all I had to do was put her up in the hotel and then get her home. Hell, since she was at loose ends, I could even give her a job in any of the hotels she wanted to work in. We had hotels all over the world; she could actually go wherever she wanted to. Quite literally.

I wouldn't disclose most of that just yet though. I knew she'd want to escape the minute she saw the hotel, when she saw the staff rooms; she'd probably want to ask me a few dozen more questions before she ran. We owned one of the most expensive hotels in London. Even our staff rooms were quality. She might be down on her luck, but the tilt to her chin told me this girl had pride. She wouldn't want to take my charity, and only had so far because she was hungry and tired.

I could already hear how tired she was in the way her steps slowed, so I knew I'd be able to convince her to stay at least one night. That would keep her off the streets for that long anyway. I had to fly back to America in the morning, but I'd keep her warm and safe for tonight at least. I'd have Mason arrange something for her the next day; my brother was good at stuff like that. Both of my brothers were preoccupied with their new women, but I knew Mason would squeeze that in for me if I asked.

My elder brothers, both blond with gray eyes, were so different from me with their coloring, but we had the same face, all three of us. We were our father's sons, after all.

"Oh!" I heard her gasp as I tugged at her hand when we

reached the hotel. I couldn't help a smirk when her eyes went round and her mouth dropped open as her head tilted back.

"I thought…" she started, but shut her mouth.

"You thought it was a Holiday Inn, maybe?" I teased her, and she looked at me with eyes full of doubt.

"I can't go in there. It's too nice. I don't have… and I look… Oh, thank you, but no." She tried to pull away, but I wouldn't let her.

"You can, and you will. I don't often drag women in off the street, but when I do…" I knew it was the wrong thing to say, and her eyes filled with tears to prove it.

I'd dated models and waitresses, I'd dated princesses and store clerks; I wasn't a picky kind of guy. Nor was I a snob. What I was, however, was thoughtless. "Look, I'm sorry, I know that came out utterly wrong. I meant, I'm not often given the chance to give back, to use what I have for real good. If you let me help you, you'll be doing me a favor."

"What?" she asked, and I knew she was confused because so was I.

"My dad says I'm a selfish jerk and need to learn the value of hard work. So he's making me work in the hotels. If I let you stay here, free, with no strings attached, then I've proven to myself I'm not selfish, right? Which in itself may be selfish, hmm." I stopped and thought about it for a moment, but dismissed it; it didn't matter. "Either way, I'm not about to let you go back out on the street. Especially without your cheese sticks."

"Fingers," she said, a twitch at the corner of her lips.

"Pardon?" Now I really was confused.

"Well, they call fish sticks fish fingers here. Shouldn't they call cheese sticks cheese fingers?" Her brown eyes filled with mirth this time, and I knew I'd won.

"You're quite right, my dear. Come on now, in you go." I tugged at our joined hands, and she followed me in.

I grabbed a few things from a supply closet, found an empty staff room in the computer system, and headed to the fifth floor where the room was. It was a wing we hadn't renovated this year, but it was still resoundingly posh. White walls, cream carpet, and tasteful gold accents made the floor a dream to walk through sometimes. There were no distracting colors or tasteless paintings. Just pure, creamy white everything.

The door opened to her quarters to reveal a small sitting room with a television, a small but full kitchen, and a bedroom with a bathroom in the back. I handed her the bag and showed her around.

"Could I?" she started as she looked in and saw a white robe with the name of the hotel.

"Shower? Of course, my dear. I'll leave you if you'd like and let you have some rest."

"No!" she called out, her eyes panicked as she looked around. "I, just, I."

"Too wound up to be alone? I'll call for some room service, shall I? Have a few things brought up." She paused, her eyes full of tears again, and I smiled softly. "Go on. I'll be here when you come out."

You would think she'd be terrified of being alone with me, but she seemed to have that instant connection with me that I did with her. Who knew, maybe she'd rob the place blind and run off in the night, but something told me she wouldn't. There was something about her that reminded me of a scared rabbit, and I knew she'd be right here in the morning, and if not, she wouldn't have taken anything I didn't explicitly offer.

She didn't show the signs of a drug addict, or a scrounger, just a woman down on her luck. She took a deep breath, and then she went into the bathroom. I heard the lock click quietly and smiled to myself. She was a sensible woman then.

I've played the field, don't get me wrong; I love women. I wasn't the kind of man who needed to force himself on a woman or extort her for sex, and I didn't want to. I wouldn't turn down a chance to find out what she hid beneath that coat of hers, but I wasn't about to intimate that to her, at all.

I heard the shower turn on and within moments I heard a sigh as the smell of soap filled the air from the crack under the door. I'd put plenty of soap, shampoo, conditioner, lotion, a toothbrush, toothpaste, a brush, and deodorant in the bag. Things people sometimes forgot and often ran out of on trips, and we kept a supply so guests wouldn't have to run out and get them at an awkward moment.

I heard her hum as the water ran, and I smiled. She was content. I went to the phone and got room service. I ordered coffee for the pot in the room, tea, milk, sugar, some pots of jam and bread, and a few doughnuts in case she got peckish in the night. I also ordered a few savory dishes she could pop in the microwave and had them all in order by the time she came out. The robe was tucked around her, and she'd brushed her hair out but hadn't dried it.

The room was warm, and her skin glowed from the heat of her shower. "All better?"

"Oh, that was heaven!" She looked at the bags of coffee on the counter and looked at me. "Would you like some?"

"If you feel like it. Or I can go." She'd spotted the doughnuts and tucked into one before I'd even answered her. She was hungry.

"No, I've been alone and haven't spoken to anyone for days now. It's nice to have someone around." Her eyes still looked strained, but her body was more relaxed now. "I've been terrified, here alone."

"I imagine you were. Well, I think we can soon get you sorted." The coffee was done and in mugs by the time we moved into the sitting room.

"This was more than enough. I'll be gone first thing in the morning." She waved her hand around the room, her eyes still tired around the corners.

The two lights on the end table were all that was on, and up here, high in the air, you couldn't hear the noise outside. The room was calm, warm, and safe. "You'll stay right here, Ember. This is a staff room that isn't being used anyway, so you can stay as long as you need to. Room service has been told to bring you whatever you ask for, and well, I suppose we'll have to find you some clothes."

I hadn't meant it to sound like I'd noticed, but it was hard not to. Ember's smooth legs, still tan from her summer in the sun, were on display and the gap at the top of the robe told me she was naked underneath it. I had to admit though, she looked rather young without her cap and stress around her eyes.

"How old are you, Ember?" I tilted my head, and she followed suit.

"I'm twenty-one, why? How old are you?" Her lips parted slightly as she spoke, and her pupils went wide as she looked at me.

"I'm twenty-four." *Old enough to know better,* my brain told me. I hadn't wanted sex from her, and she'd been afraid I would at one point in the evening.

Now, alone and relaxed, her eyes showed an interest that said we'd both been wrong. "I should probably go."

"Do you have to?" Something in her voice changed, became sultry, and I shifted on the couch. That voice had almost broken me.

"I should."

"After coffee. It's the least I can do," she said and pointed her head at the table where both mugs were going cold.

She curled up into her end of the couch and turned on the television. "I'm sorry if I offended you."

"No, it's not that. I just don't want you to feel obligated. Truly, I'm not that kind of guy."

"I know. Something tells me you aren't like any man I've ever met before." She gave a yawn then, and her head rested on the back of the couch. In seconds she was asleep.

I watched her, the coffee forgotten once more, and wondered how any man could treat such an angelic creature as she'd been treated. A man on drugs, no doubt, because Ember was beautiful, but she was also good. I'd known that from the moment I'd laid eyes on her. She was good.

Quite unlike most women I knew. It wasn't the hotel that had made desire flare in those eyes of her. It might have been desperation after her split with this tosser she'd left behind, but I didn't think it was that. I wasn't a rebound for her either. No, there was something between us, something that screamed connection in my mind, but didn't make sense to me.

I'd been sexually active a long time. Far longer than I should have been, probably, and I knew women. They slept with me because they found me attractive, or because some wanted to try to seduce me into marriage. Others knew the game and knew it was fuck and nothing more. Ember wasn't any of those things.

I found her desirable. From the voracious way she'd eaten, to the way she'd hummed at the pleasure of a shower, to the adorable way she'd curled up on the end of the couch; she was desirable. Her body was incredible, and now that she wasn't hidden under layers, I could see that. She had firm, high breasts, a nice curve to her waist, and wide hips with thighs a man could hang on to. But those eyes were her most desirable feature. They said things she probably hadn't even realized she'd thought. I was in trouble, and I knew it. But for the first time in my selfish life, I didn't run away from the trouble of her kind. I wanted to stay right where I was.

4

EMBER

Ember

My brain was too exhausted to think. I didn't want to be alone. In all my life, even when Mom was at her worst with the drugs, I'd not been alone. And when Graham had given me the silent treatment until my will broke and I gave in to whatever it was he wanted, I'd not been alone. Not until this week, in that room at night, terrified of what could happen because there was nobody there to keep me safe.

Even now, this stranger with seductive eyes and a kind voice was better than solitude. I'd barely spoken to anyone in the days I was on the street, and now, even if we didn't talk, it was nice to have someone there. I was safe here, once the door was locked it would be hard for someone to get in, but I still didn't want to be alone. That was why I gravitated toward parks so often. They were full of people and sounds.

The television on the nightly news reports, a full stomach, and the warm robe lulled me into sleep. Softly the sounds died away, my breath evened out, and I forgot how nice it was to use toothpaste and have clean teeth as sleep came for me. Everything just… faded.

Until Kevin woke me up. I startled, my arms went out to fend off whoever it was that had touched me, and a sound escaped my throat. I didn't know what the sound was, it could have been a word, but whatever it was, the combination made Kevin jump back and say my name softly.

"It's alright, Ember. It's okay." The sound of the name reminded me of where I was. I'd always hated my real name, but I did wonder what it would sound like in that old-fashioned accent of his. I bet it would sound nice growled into my ear…

I was already on my way back to sleep, but Kevin's soft fingers on my face woke me up again. "Come on, lass, get in bed why don't you?"

"What?" I felt my eyebrows scrunch as I looked into his eyes. So self-assured, so very certain of the world around him. I wished I had that kind of security. I'd never had it though, so there was no use wishing for it now.

"Get in bed. You need to rest."

Something in me, some part that didn't want to be alone, made me do something really desperate then. "Don't leave."

The words were a breath from my lips as my arms went

around his neck, and I pulled him down to kiss him. I'd never in my life initiated a kiss. Not even with Graham. I did then though, and I wasn't sorry either. Not when it felt so nice to have his lips on mine.

"Ember…" he said softly, as he tried to pull away.

"You don't want me?" I asked, not an accusation, just curiosity.

"I do, but… this isn't the right time for you." I could see regret in his eyes and wondered if it was because he wished he could take the words back, or because he regretted what I'd done.

"I may never have the chance again. It's the perfect time." I pulled him down then and opened my mouth to flick my tongue along his lips.

I didn't know what came over me. One minute I was the diminutive angel, the next a seductress, but whatever it was didn't want to stop. I kissed him long and deep, and when his resistance caved he pressed his chest into mine to deepen the kiss, and we moaned together.

Maybe it was the fact that he seemed stable, self-possessed, confident, all of the things that Graham wasn't. Graham had the confidence that low self-esteem gave him, bravado that could melt with the slightest word or look into rage as he tried to defend the wall he'd built around himself long before I came along. A wall that left him little more than a petulant child. But here, this man, Kevin, he was all the things a man should be, and I wanted that, if for nothing more than the moment he'd give me.

"I want this. Not because you fed me, or gave me a place to stay; this isn't payment for services rendered. I need this.

I need you." I looked into his eyes and saw the uncertainty melt away. Something like surprise shown in his eyes, but he smothered it when he closed his eyelids and kissed me.

Then we both forgot everything except the pursuit of pleasure.

He settled between my thighs, a light pressure against my core, and I sighed into his mouth. My fingers sought to remove the crisp white button-up shirt he wore, and buttons left their holes as if that was all they'd ever wanted to do. Then his pants were gone, and silky flesh replaced the feel of silk cloth against my center. I wore only the robe and a brush of his hand made the panels open.

He didn't just plunge into me eagerly, though that was what I expected. I'd become used to that frantic need to just get it over with, before I was left with an ache that wouldn't be satisfied. No, this man took his time, despite being pressed into me in a very intimate place. Instead of just fucking me, he gazed down at the body he'd revealed with patient fingers.

His fingers traced the outline of my collarbone as his eyes squinted in appreciation. He looked intrigued, and I wondered if he'd ever been with a woman with some weight to her. He was delighted though, I could see it in the way his eyes lit up. I'd gained weight in Britain, and luckily, he'd saved me before I managed to lose too much of it because of Graham's cold-hearted callousness.

He swept thoughts of the other man away when his lips touched the flat plane just below my collarbone. Gently, his fingers roamed that space until I was breathless with fascination. What would he do next?

I reached for his shoulders and my back arched when his fingers traced over a light pink nipple that had turned a darker color with my excitement. My heart pounded in my chest, and I wanted to move my hips, to force the moment when he was inside of me, but he just soothed me with a soft sound and let his lips take the place of his fingers.

Heat, wet and so good, encircled the bud, but his hands didn't stop. They traveled down my ribs, down the right side of my waist, over my hips. For a moment I couldn't breathe. Anticipation mixed with the pleasure he had already given me, he was going to touch me there. He was going to make me come. Things the other had stopped doing so long ago.

I could have screamed with the excitement that had started to build. This was going to be so worth it. My day had started off so bleak, but now, it might just be the best day of my life. Ever. I pulled my hips back when his hand probed between our bodies and waited, breath held. Would he really? *Oh please, touch me there, please touch me there!*

My brain was frantic, and so was my body as my hips curled toward him, toward that probing hand. And when he found me?

His lips tugged harder at my nipple, and I couldn't think of anything but how good it felt to have his fingers on me. The ache inside of me built, and little sparks shot out from my center, from the spot that had been neglected far too often.

"Are you sure you want this, Ember?" My name on his lips was an aphrodisiac, and I wanted to hear him say it again. But he'd asked me a question.

"You're, you know, touching me, Kevin. Do you think I'd let you do that if I wasn't sure?" I was surprised I could put that many words together in a sentence, but proud that I had managed it.

"No, I mean are you sure you want me to make you come?" His fingers didn't stop the slow stroke on my clit. They increased the pressure slightly, and I forgot to breathe. "Ember? Are you sure you want me to fuck you? Because that's how this is going to end, and I need to know that now. I need to know you're going to let me inside of you."

"Yes. Please. I want…" I looked up at him, my hips now moved to the rhythm of his fingers and my fingers were clutched into his shoulder blades. He had a wide, muscular chest and his back was just as broad. The silky skin there invited fingernails, long ones, to dig in.

"You want what, Ember?" he demanded, and I opened the eyes I'd only just shut.

"I want you to make me come. I want you to fuck me, Kevin. I want you to make me yours." I breathed the last words against his lips, he was that close. I flicked a tongue out to tempt him closer, and he closed his mouth over mine.

His fingers still worked at me, and I was close, so close. One of my hands moved down to his arm, to grasp at the ropes of muscle there, to guide him, to beg him not to stop. And he didn't; he kept up the slick flick of his finger over that delicious spot until I felt my hips go tight and my back began to arch, so close... just a little more.

The world turned to black as his hand moved over me,

an intimate touch of a stranger who knew exactly what I needed. I felt the heat spread through me, up into my abdomen, a heat that turned into pleasure as my brain exploded, and my muscles convulsed. My heels dug into the couch, my thighs clamped around him, and my hips twisted as I felt the relief of release.

I didn't breathe, I just felt as the waves continued, until I thought I'd die from it all. This was the single most exquisite moment of my life. Then it all started over again and harsh noise tore from my throat.

"That's it, Ember. Take what you deserve." His lips traced down my neck and I gulped for air, my eyes open but unseeing. All I was in that moment was pleasure, and I could hear the satisfaction in his voice. "I so want to fuck you."

That set me off again and my short fingernails dug into his arm, and I realized only then that I still clutched at it. I felt the thud of my pulse in my head, in my neck, but didn't care if my heart gave out right then. This was perfection. Heat made my skin slick, and I wanted water, but I didn't want this to stop.

What else could this man give me?

When the waves began to ebb slightly, he pulled away, stood, and picked me up from the couch. In strong arms, I wrapped my own around his neck, and he kissed me as he carried me to the bed. He was naked, somehow his shoes were gone, and he was completely bare.

"Condom?" I asked, my tongue clumsy and untrustworthy, but it managed that word.

"Here." His hand tightened around my thigh, and I felt the foil packet.

"Good." I'd had birth control pills when we came here, but I was almost out. I didn't even know how to get something like that here. I needed to go home, but not yet. Not until he'd lit me up one more time.

He laid me on the bed, and I sprawled out to take him in my arms. My thighs fell open without direction, and he came up between them.

I still hadn't seen all of him, but I'd felt him, thick and hard between my thighs. I knew there was more than enough there to do the job. My hands ran up the ridges of his stomach muscles, over his ribs, and spread out over his chest as he leaned up to kiss me. He pulled away to put the condom on, and then he was back.

Need rose again as he moved down my body, his hands lingered in some spots, but brushed over others. Until he was there. I felt hot air that turned cool before it found my damp skin. Was he going to… "Fuck."

I groaned the word as his tongue slid up my folds until he found that spot again. So many men didn't have an idea where the clit was, but it was like Kevin had a homing beacon directing him right to it. I felt his tongue flat over it before his lips sucked and blew my mind.

I was on cloud nine and didn't want to get off of it. My hands went over my face, to hide the world, because I couldn't do anything else to smother my scream of delight. I heard this loud groan and then I felt my chest rumble as I responded in kind. Kevin obviously enjoyed what he had found between my thighs.

My hands tangled in his hair, and I rode his face until I'd burst into blackness all over again. That's when he slid into me, when I was totally oblivious, and I'd reached the stars. He thrust into me, and I saw a look of pure delight on his face in the short moment when I blinked, just before I closed my eyes to concentrate on the sensation of his cock as it stretched me, filled me to touch every aching inch of me.

I wanted to ride him, but I'd take what he offered. We found the perfect pace, and when my hands found his hair and pulled his head back, he groaned my name.

I'd never heard anything more erotic.

"Follow me, come with me, Ember."

That's when something completely new happened. I felt myself explode, a convulsion of muscles that spasmed around him as he groaned my name all over again.

He continued to drive into me, until the moment when I gasped a breath at last. Then he fell beside me, tucked me into his body, and held me until I couldn't stay awake anymore. I fell asleep in his arms, in the arms of a man unlike any I had ever known. Sexy, articulate, a little bit of a cheeky monkey at times I'd guessed, but more than that, he was one thing I'd never known in a man. Kind. Kevin was kind, and that was totally new to me.

5

EMBER

Ember

Sunlight cut through the window and straight into the bedroom the next morning. I reached out, wondered if he'd stayed with me, but the bed was empty. I let out a sigh of disappointment, but also, of relief. No awkward morning-after conversation. I sprawled out beneath the luxury quality duvet and sighed.

What had I done to deserve this? I wondered how long I could stay. A pang of hunger reminded me he'd said I could stay as long as I wanted, could order anything I wanted from room service. I sighed again, happily, and turned the television on to a music channel as I decided to get out of bed and shower. An old song, Rock Me Gently by Andy Kim, started as I stepped into the water completely naked.

Kevin had kept me up until dawn, and I sang along as I soaped up my hair. I could have cried I was so happy. I didn't know if I'd see Mr. Kevin Thompson ever again, but I knew one thing. I'd never been loved quite like that before, and yeah, I wanted a repeat. Whether I'd get it was another matter altogether. I wrapped myself in a towel and sang as I exited the bathroom.

I'd developed a taste for odd songs that the pubs would play, usually really old rock songs that hadn't quite made it to America but should have. I was a singer, I loved songs of all genres really, but this stuff from the 60s and 70s was sexy and also made me giggle a lot. A new song came on, and I smiled. This one had made it across the pond. Exile, Kiss You All Over. I sank down onto the bed and sang along as I replayed the night before in my mind.

Yeah, the song was accurate. I wanted to do all of those things we'd done, all over again, only I didn't care if it was night or day. I just wanted to feel those things he'd made me feel, to explore him a lot more than I had the night before. Although, that second time, I'd done a little more. I'd actually managed to get my hand down between us, to wrap my fingers around him until he'd distracted me with kisses along my neck as he thrust himself into me.

It had been incredible. Every single moment from when I looked up to see he watched me as I sang, until I'd woke up this morning had been incredible. My future was still uncertain, but with some sleep, food, a hot shower, and some fantastic sex, I didn't feel so lost. Yet.

I bit the inside of my lip as I thought about what the future might hold. I didn't have many options, not many at all, and this wasn't going to be easy. I glanced over at the things room service had brought in the night before and saw a note there.

"I had to leave early, my father is ill," Kevin had written. I liked his handwriting; it was rather English from what I'd seen so far. "Call my brother, Mason. He'll be able to help you. I've already called to tell him he's to give you whatever you need. Thanks for last night, I hope to see you again."

He hoped to see me again. Maybe not a one-night stand then? A knock at the door drew my attention away from the note. I went to the door and a staff member from the hotel was there. "These are for you."

I took the bags from the young man, and he promptly left. I looked in the bags and found some clothes and a brand new phone. I smiled at the phone; it was the latest version of a phone I'd never been able to afford before. It would work outside of Britain and was unlocked so I could put a US SIM card in it when I got back there. I danced in place with glee. The man was so sweet!

I threw the clothes on the bed and started the process of getting the phone set up. Another knock at the door and a plane ticket was brought to me. For a minute, I wondered if last night had been that good. But then, I remembered Kevin had said he'd take care of getting me back home before we'd done the deed. This was just kindness, pure and simple. I looked at the date on the ticket. Tomorrow. I'd be going home tomorrow! Thank goodness, that was before my time was up!

I got the phone on finally and within seconds it

vibrated. I had a call, but who would be calling me? "Hello?"

"Miss Jones, I presume?" a rather stiff, but almost familiar voice came over the line.

"Yes, who is this?" Always blunt, that was me. I pushed my hair out of my face and stared at the walls as I waited.

"I am Mason Thompson. My brother asked me to contact you. I've bought you a ticket for a flight that will bring you to our hotel in Charlotte, and have ordered the phone and clothes he asked for." The voice on the other end was cold, uncaring, and I wondered how the two men could sound so different? "Is there anything else you require?"

"I… not that I know of." I gulped and wondered if this had gone too far now. He'd arranged for me to have a room at the hotel in Charlotte too? He'd thought of everything then. Everything except a job.

"Good, then I wish you a good day, miss." The line went dead, and I stared at the phone. My heart had raced the entire time I was on the phone, but I took a deep breath to calm it down.

Then I remembered Graham. Would he make it back to America? Would he hunt me down, even there? My heart raced at the thought. The man was such a bastard! He'd dragged me to a new country, tried to make me sell drugs, and I knew if he found me that would be the end for me. I bit the inside of my lip and stared at the door. He couldn't find me here, never in a million years would he find me here.

I doubt he'd find me in Charlotte either. He'd expect me

to go back to Alabama or to Kentucky, maybe, but not to North Carolina. I'd be safe, as long as he didn't read my social media. Graham didn't trust things like Facebook or Twitter though. It was just the man trying to keep tabs on us, he'd always said in a voice that made him sound incredibly stupid. I'd tried to ignore his obsession with conspiracy theories, but when he outright dropped the words from his mouth it was hard to ignore.

That was all done now, I counted my blessings. At least the way he'd dropped me had ensured I'd never go back to him. I wasn't even that heartbroken over the end of it all, though I should have been. He'd been my first everything. I was sad, certainly, hurt that he'd treated me so badly, but he'd always been a jerk. I'd just overlooked it because at least someone had said they loved me. I didn't have time for that now. I had to plan a new life, in a new city, with no car, no formal address, and no way of making money.

I decided to stay in the room, just in case, until it was time for me to go. I went through the bags again and found a backpack that would hold my meager possessions and a few other things I might need. Somebody had thought of everything I might need then. I still had the money that had been thrown into my guitar case before Kevin came along. That would cover bus fare to the airport. I could take lunch and a couple bottles of water from here for the wait at the airport.

That meant I had an entire day with nothing to do then. I looked around and couldn't find much to do. My thoughts returned to Kevin, and I glanced at the phone. I could look him up. I picked it up, scrolled around, and typed Kevin's name into the search engine. I found a few other Kevin Thompsons, but found him without any problems.

His smile separated him from all the rest. He actually had a Wiki page too! I scrolled through and saw his family was beyond my wildest dreams wealthy, and the endearing young man I'd met had quite the education. He'd been to the most prestigious boarding school in Britain, a place called Charterhouse, and had gone to university at Cambridge.

Holy shit! The man wasn't just kind and sexy, but he was also intelligent. Very, to have attended Cambridge! That intimidated me a little. I wasn't stupid, but I'd barely managed to graduate high school. I'd had no illusions about college or a future when I was a teenager, and my grades had reflected that. Kevin had attended Cambridge though. A university in Britain that even I'd heard of!

Sheesh! Who was this guy?

I felt a smile tug at my lips when I saw he'd been in a band during his college years. He'd played guitar and the drums. I wondered what kind of music it was they played and went back to reading. Ah, they'd played music similar to that of the Lumineers. An odd choice for a band based in Britain, but then again, perhaps not. It was the new alternative music, wasn't it? A mix of country and rock.

I wondered if he'd sung too. I could just picture a younger Kevin, his eyes closed as he sang along to a song. My heart gushed, and I fell back into the bed. I didn't think I'd ever felt that emotion before, that sort of school-girl-crush that put me in mind of a word I'd never quite understood before. Squee! A made-up word, one that expressed something I'd only just been able to get.

Squee was the perfect word for it.

Damn, maybe I was taking this too far. It wasn't like I'd ever see him again, not once I got back to America. I bet he dated models usually; I'd been nothing more than a moment of weakness. A walk on the wild side. I went through more web pages and found that Kevin had dated, and plenty, but not all of the women were models, or thin and blonde. Some were normal women with normal jobs.

He was a bit of a sportsman, which explained his well-sculpted body, and he spent a lot of time working with charities. So what he'd done for me wasn't so out of character then.

I learned a little bit about his brothers too. Trent the eldest and a bit of a dick from what I'd read. Unapproach-able and always in control, he took self-possessed to a new height. Then there was Mason, the one I'd talked to. He was, from all reports, a man who never turned down a chance to party. I couldn't really find out how he fit into the hotel's staff, but did he have to with that kind of family wealth?

Mason had sounded as cold as Trent was supposed to be on the phone, but I saw he was more like Kevin than Trent. He played sports too, rugby at one point, where Kevin played polo, but he hadn't followed that career for some reason. Oh well, it wasn't important. I flicked off the tabloid website and looked for a movie to watch. I didn't need to know everything about these people, but I knew something about them now.

Mainly, they weren't sex-traffickers so I wasn't getting myself into anything shady. *Would that be on a tabloid site though?* I wondered as I headed into the kitchen to make some toast and scrambled eggs. I saw a bottle of white wine in the fridge that I would definitely have a go at later on tonight.

I tripped on my guitar case as I walked back into the living room, but I managed to not set the kitchen on fire. That was a miracle. I wasn't the best cook in the world, and my brush with the guitar case wasn't my first. I could be clumsy sometimes. My mom always said I needed glasses because I could trip over thin air, but how would glasses help improve that? My eyes had been tested anyway, and they'd been fine.

I brushed my hair out of my face and settled on the couch to eat. I felt a twinge of soreness and smirked. That was new, but it wasn't a bad thing. Kevin had been thick and long. I wouldn't have minded a bit if he'd still been here this morning, but beggars couldn't be choosers. Besides, his note had said his father was ill. I couldn't blame him for leaving, could I?

I munched on toast and my eggs and waited for the day to pass. I didn't want to go outside; something might fuck up this opportunity I'd been given, and I had nothing else to do. I found a free book online and opened it on my new phone, determined to enjoy the luxury of a king-size bed all to myself. I snuggled down and began to read, still amazed at how much had changed in less than twenty-four hours.

Yesterday, I'd basically been begging in the park. Today

I was in a hotel I could never hope to afford, and the world had shown me a kindness I didn't know existed anymore. Well, Kevin Thompson had. I'd made a mistake when I decided to come to England with Graham, but somehow, fate had decided to turn that into a very good decision. I wasn't going to argue with that.

I'd be careful, I'd tread wisely, but I'd also take the hand that had been held out to me. It would be stupid to do otherwise. Even if I never saw Kevin again, this would have all been worth it. I had this new thought in my head, a new idea. Maybe humanity wasn't all bad.

6

───

KEVIN

Kevin

I scraped a hand over my jaw and knew I needed to shave off the beard I'd grown recently, but I was too exhausted. A night with Ember, a transatlantic flight, and dealing with a shitstorm at home had left me with little time to rest. I hadn't even had time to eat yet. I'd hidden in a bathroom at our Charlotte branch for the time being. I just needed a moment to myself.

I wasn't normally around at our offices in the States; I preferred to stay on the other side of the Atlantic, but the message said Dad was ill. I couldn't stay away, could I? There was always too much tension in the air when I was at home, and I liked to avoid that. I liked to keep peace and calm in my private life, even if I couldn't have it in my work life. Especially because of that, actually.

I scrolled through my phone, my feet on the wall ahead of me. The bathroom was one of the luxury numbers for upper management, and I had sat in the leather chair in one corner, my feet propped up as I tried to fight off the urge to sleep. Thoughts of Ember flashed in my mind, and I smiled. She'd snored softly when I kissed her goodbye this morning.

She was one incredible, determined woman, Ember Jones. And sexy as fuck too. Her body was lush, and I'd loved every moment of my discovery of her. I swear, I could still taste her on my tongue. I didn't even try to stop the smirk that spread over my face then. She'd been all I could have hoped for and then some. The way she sighed my name just as she came, and the way her back arched when I thrust into her were all seared into my memory.

My phone chirped, and I swiped the message from my eldest brother away. Fuck Trent. Fuck Mason. Fuck Dad if he didn't want to see any of us. Why had I flown across the Atlantic if he didn't want to see me after I got here? Rubbish, that's what this was. But soon, Ember would be back.

That would make this worth it. Tomorrow she'd be in Charlotte, late, but still here. I couldn't wait to see her. I could barely get her off of my mind. Even if Trent already had jobs for me to do. I'd do them, it was my duty as my father's son to help take care of his empire, but for the rest of the night they could all piss off.

I sighed, stood, and straightened my clothes. I wanted to call Ember, but it was late here in America; it would be extremely late in London. It had been a fucker of a day.

The flight, the confusion when Dad wouldn't see me, and here at the hotel, where Trent had already started with his demands, and I was fairly certain Mason had already set up a party. He always did.

I chuckled and headed to my room. I should have just gone back to the house, but it was more convenient to stay here in the family quarters. I hadn't told Ember the exact truth about the suite she was in. It was a staff suite, yes, but it was for family more than staff. I knew she'd have refused and demanded one of the less costly rooms.

I knew she'd received all of the packages I'd arranged, and that she'd soon be out of the country that hadn't shown her many kindnesses. I'd have to change that for her one day and show her just how wonderful London was when you were there with the right people. I headed for the kitchen area once I'd reached my rooms and pulled out a bottle of water. I shrugged out of the suit jacket I'd had on for far too long today and slipped the buttons loose on the light blue shirt I wore underneath.

I kicked off my shoes and headed into the bathroom. After a shower and a fresh shave, I dressed in a long-sleeved gray v-neck sweater and a pair of dark blue jeans. I headed into the living room and ordered room service, and then sat down to wait at the piano. My room was the only one with a piano. My fingers tapped out a tune as I thought about Ember. Ember whose real name was Bridget Jones. That poor woman.

I felt a smile cross my lips and stroked the keys with fingers that were sure of the tune now. I wasn't surprised to find I'd recreated the song Ember had sung only hours before. I was as musical as she was, some even said talented when it came to the piano, but my band days were over. I still liked to play the piano and the drums, but these days my fingers tapped at keyboard keys far more than at the ivory keys of my piano.

I lost myself in the memory of notes, in her voice, the serenity of her face as she'd sung about loss and happiness, a song that had lit her face up with the memories it evoked. I had to make that girl a star, somehow. She had the voice for it.

And I had a bar that needed a singer. My fingers continued as I developed the plan in my mind. I could install her there, she'd have rooms of her own, a job, and the protection of hotel security. And I knew a few people in the music industry who might be interested in her. Yes, this might work.

I stopped playing when my food came to the door and sat down on the couch to wait for her to arrive. A car would pick her up from the airport and I'd meet her later, when she came back to me. I didn't plan to fall asleep after I ate; it just happened.

This wasn't the life I'd planned so long ago. I'd once had the desire to be a musician, but businessman with a family and responsibilities seemed to be the path my friends had taken. Some were serious partiers, but they'd now settled down and become family men. I'd never wanted a child, not until I saw how my friends looked at their new babies. There was something there I wanted. Something that I envied them for, and I'd never felt that before.

My thoughts were on those things when I leaned my

head against the arm of the black leather couch. Music played softly from the television, and my thoughts drifted lulling me into a dreamy sleep. I pictured Ember with a baby bump, and then a child in her arms. Her sweet face, so sensual when I kissed her, so eager when we talked about her music, would be filled with that look I'd seen so many times on others.

And my baby would be in her arms.

An ache formed in my chest unlike anything I'd ever felt before. Deep and painful, it burned out to my stomach and across my chest as I walked toward them. My hand went into her hair, and she smiled at me. Fuck, my heart swelled, and I fell to my knees in front of her. She was seated beneath the sprawling oak tree in my family's estate, sunlight a beam around her.

"I knew you'd bring me to life." I wasn't sure what the words meant, but I said them.

Her brown eyes, a dark but clear brown, pierced into me, and I felt as if she'd wrapped the sunlight around my soul. I sank down, my fingers now on the head of the child in her arms, our child. Tiny green eyes looked up at me, and something shifted in my chest. Our baby.

"Ember... I..." I couldn't say it though because she kissed me instead. I placed my hands on her shoulders and let the kiss carry on.

How she'd managed to give me so much happiness was a mystery, but there it was.

The dream shifted, and I was alone in a dark room. A woman with black hair sat in a chair and waited for me to strip the black wrap dress off of her, but I turned back to

Ember, to the light she'd promised. I called out Ember's name, reached for her, and felt terror as the woman in the black leather chair pulled me to her with some invisible beam. I fought and screamed until I woke myself up.

Sunlight poured through the windows, and the world was silent. The television had gone off as I slept. I looked at the clock that hung on the wall and groaned. I'd missed Ember!

I went into the bathroom, determined to go see her, even if it meant I'd have to wake her up. Trent had other plans, though, and he'd already sent me a dozen messages by the time I got out of the shower. He needed some paper in the office, and I sent him a message to tell him where they were. He still couldn't find them so I decided to fetch the damned papers so he'd leave me alone and then go find Ember.

"Hey, this woman you've got Mason catering to, what is she to you?" Trent asked as soon as I walked into the office. Bright sunlight streamed in through the wall of glass behind Trent, and I blinked.

"What?" I asked, my patience thin. Why did he think he was the boss here? Because he was the oldest? He could suck my...

"The woman, who is she?"

"None of your business," I said with a hint of a sneer and went to find the papers he'd asked for.

"Fine, whatever. Thanks, I need you to take on some work while you're here, Kevin. Dad's had the reins so long, but we have to figure out his system. He should have brought you two into check a long time ago."

I stood there, an eyebrow lifted as my eldest brother insulted me. I doubted he even meant to, but he did. He always did. I rolled my eyes softly, adjusted my jaw to a place where it wasn't clenched so tight, and breathed in to let the annoyance go. "What do you need me to do, Trent? I have plans today."

"We need to try to see Dad again. Your plans can wait." He shoved papers against my chest as he walked past me and his desk. "Find out what those are about and let me know."

"I, what? Trent? You have to give me a little more than that for instructions." I looked down at the crumpled report he'd slapped against my chest and tried to make sense of the title on the cover. "Trent, this is stuff Dad never let us deal with. We can't… he'll be back to work in a few days…"

"No, he's going to be out for quite a while. We have to take over for now. And not let his empire crumple around us. Figure that out and get back to me. You know as much as I do at this point."

I sat and looked over the report. I'd talk to Ember later. She was probably asleep anyway, right? I'd obviously needed sleep, so I knew she probably did too. That trip across the Atlantic could be rough on you. Maybe I could take lunch to her room and we could…

Trent gave a frustrated growl, and I looked up to watch him pick up the desk phone, punch in numbers, and bark something at somebody. Then he stood and left the office. I didn't bother to ask where he'd gone. It wasn't important. I put the report down and went over to look at the pile of papers, files, and other detritus on the desk.

This was my father's desk, his office, and we'd been left to just get on with it. What was my father playing at here? We didn't even know for sure what was wrong with him, and all of the information we received about him came through our sister, Emily. My father wasn't above trickery when it came to his children. Was this all a game to him, some effort of his to bring us together for some reason?

I thought about my siblings as people I knew but didn't really want to be around most of the time. Trent always had some kind of superiority complex. He was the first born, and that made the rest of us illegitimate in his eyes. We were the children of his stepmother, things to be ignored because we weren't of the royal line, or so it seemed to me.

Mason was carefree, the eldest of my mother's children, but the first to invade Trent's space. He had a way of letting Trent's nastiness roll off his back. Emily had that knack too. She could just sweet talk Trent, or our father for that matter, into doing whatever was best. Or she'd just bluntly tell them how they'd fucked up and what they needed to do to fix it. Emily was our little sister, but she was also a hub for all of us, and we kind of circled each other around her.

Emily made me smile with her antics, and I adored her. My mother really made someone special with that girl. Poor Mom, so many thought she was just a gold digger, but she really did love my father. I wasn't sure why she did sometimes, but she did.

I knew I had my father's arrogance, to an extent, and

his way of rolling over problems that people had. Like I had with Ember, to an extent. She had major problems, and instead of giving her money to let her fix those problems, I'd dealt with it. I found it easier to just eliminate the problems that could be dealt with than to wait for others to figure out how to do it. I supposed Emily and I all had inherited that trait from our father.

I went back to work on the report after that little reverie, a little perplexed at where the whole thing had come from. It was kind of like that dream of Ember I'd had. I had never considered settling down with one woman, though it had seemed to hold a little appeal lately, and when I'd seen her, something deep inside said, that's it. She's the one. Which is part of the reason I'd just taken away all of her problems without even consulting her about them.

She was the one, I knew it down to my toes. What amazed me was, I was good with that.

7

EMBER

Ember

I strummed nimble fingers over the strings of my guitar and stared out the window of my room. I was in America again, in a state that I've only ever driven through before, without a clue as to what to do next. I'd decided to work on a new song, but all I could think about was what I needed to do next. I was at loose ends.

"You brought me to the moon, and you took me through the stars. But when you left me there to… eat spaghetti, it tore my world apart." I laughed at myself but wrote down the lines anyway. Writing songs wasn't always serious.

It was skill I'd picked up a long time ago, but I hadn't really done anything with it. I didn't know how to get the attention of bands, singers, or record producers, though I knew people did. I wasn't sure I wanted someone else to sing my songs anyway. Although, there were a couple female singers out there who would probably do them justice.

I was proud of my work, but at the same time, my confidence wasn't strong. My skills had never really been tested, although the ones who had heard me play loved my voice and my style. That had been part of the problem while we were in England.

Legally, I wasn't allowed to work on the Visa Waiver Program, so I hadn't been able to play anywhere for money. That had been a major argument between Graham and me. He'd wanted me to play anyway, but I'd refused. Quietly at first, and then in a louder voice. He'd wanted me to put my stay there in jeopardy, but I'd been terrified to do it.

I'd never been inside of a jail cell, and I planned to keep it that way.

I frowned at the notebook where I'd written on the first page. A fresh, clean notebook, that I'd just defiled with words. I liked that the first thing I'd written had kind of turned into a joke. I was in a good place then.

My phone buzzed as I went back to the guitar, and I picked it up. The layout in the rooms in Charlotte were exactly the same as the ones in London, and I was kind of glad about that. It meant there was a coffee table of iron-work and glass in front of me and a similar but much smaller version beside me. I picked the phone up and saw it was my Twitter account. Someone had sent me a message.

"This is for you," the sender had written. I felt my face form into a puzzled look but clicked the link inside.

The link took me to a new Twitter page, one for the Thompson Hotel's Nashville Nights Bar and Grill. It was a country-themed bar, with the requisite cactus and cowboy boot neon signs, and the interior of the bar was all wood and metal, with a theme that brought to mind the frontier town watering holes with the swinging doors and can-can dancers who also served the male patrons. Cute, and within my genre, I guessed.

I was a little bit on the edge of both rock and country; maybe too much of both for some, but it was my style. I was usually a denim and hoodie kind of girl, who wore whatever shoes I could afford. I wasn't high maintenance, but I wasn't frumpy either. I was always in the middle, whatever the topic was.

I could fit in to a place like that.

Could it be possible? I bit the inside of my lip as I looked over the bar's Twitter site. How would I get there? My phone buzzed in my hand as another notification came through from someone I didn't know. It was the schedule for auditions at the bar. Then came a text message on my phone.

Travel arrangements had been made for me to fly to Nashville tonight and to audition tomorrow. "Holy shit…"

I couldn't believe it.

I hadn't heard from Kevin since I got back to America. I'd kind of thought he'd meet me at the airport, and we'd have some romantic reunion with flowers and clapping spectators, but there'd only been a driver there with my name on a sign. I'd sighed away my disappointment, and told myself he'd meet me at the hotel then. But my room had been empty.

There'd been no sign of him for two days now. I'd been left in limbo and hadn't known what to do. There'd been nobody to tell me how long I could stay at the hotel, no offer of a job, although, at this point, I'd take a job in housekeeping if it was offered to me. I didn't have a direction to go in. I had no idea what I should do, so I'd waited.

What else could I do? Freeze to death out to the streets I didn't know, or in an abandoned warehouse. I'd spent enough time on the streets in London. I huffed a sigh out as tears stung in my eyes.

He'd brought me home, at least. I'd told myself it was just a one-night stand after all, and had decided to move on. I'd used my phone to find out about welfare programs in North Carolina, but there was little to be offered. I wasn't pregnant, and I didn't have a child, so I was expected to go out and find a job. Fair enough, but I couldn't even drive! I didn't know anybody here. I'd never even been to a job interview.

I'd survived this long because I'd never been alone, until now. But not really. This message told me that. He hadn't forgotten about me.

I sent a return text to the number, but I didn't get a reply. Was it Kevin or a secretary who had sent the text?

I blew air out of my mouth and put my guitar and the phone down. Excitement started to build within me, and nervousness. I'd never performed for a job, or been interviewed for one as I'd said, but this was something I'd always wanted. I hadn't learned how to win interviewers over while I was in school, but I had learned to play a guitar, how to sing, and write music that stirred the soul. My direction had always been headed toward music. It just so happened that for years now I'd spun in place.

Fate had given me a guardian angel, even if he was one who had disappeared completely. Okay, he'd had sex with me and bailed, but look at what he'd done for me since then. I wasn't just some whore; he'd really thought I could sing, and he'd proven that to me with this. I knew he was behind it, because who else could it have been but him?

My thoughts were all over the place, and when I stood, I tripped over the strap of my backpack. It had become my purse, and I'd dropped it beside the couch when I first came in. My knee banged into the edge of the table and tears came to my eyes. Dang, another bruise!

I didn't get along with that table very well. You'd think by now I'd know to avoid the damned thing, but I'd managed six bruises between my two knees. I smiled, despite the pain, and headed to the kitchen for ice. At least there was a table for me to bang my knees into. And tonight, I was going to Nashville.

I had barely moved from my room here in Charlotte. I'd been too afraid I'd miss Kevin if he came by, and I barely knew anything about the town. I didn't have any money either so there was no reason to go out. My food and drink were provided by room service, they even had a laundry service, though I hadn't used it yet. Nashville though. Even if I didn't have any money, I'd still want to see the place.

I checked the time, ran into the bathroom to take a

shower, and then dried my hair. I stared into the mirror as I dried the curly locks carefully, otherwise they'd just frizz. I wasn't a goddess among women, but I wasn't ugly either. I was still young, and my face had a certain appeal. A slim nose that fit my features, wide, almond-shaped eyes, and a full smile combined in a way that was pleasing. I was no Kardashian, but I didn't want to be. I was certain those women spent hours plastering on their faces just to chisel it off again at night.

With a little work I might be prettier, but I was me and I'd accepted that long ago. I sighed, put on a pair of jeans I hadn't worn yet, then put on the red sweater that Kevin had sent to me. The color did amazing things for my eyes and the tan glow on my skin. *Not bad,* I thought with a smile and put my hands in the back pockets of my jeans. Not bad at all.

I started to gather all of my things from the room. I didn't plan on coming back, so I wanted to be sure I'd picked up everything. I made a sandwich and put a couple bottles of water in my bag. I looked around and knew I had everything packed. The bag was heavy, but I could manage it.

A driver came for me soon enough, and before I knew it, I was walking into the Thompson Hotel in Nashville. The sun had sunk while I was in the sky, and the hotel was lit up to fight off the night. It was a tasteful place, modern and expensive looking with wood accents, dark brown carpeting, and gold accents here and there. I walked in, told the receptionist my name, and was given a room key.

"Thanks," I said to her and went up to my room. As I

suspected, exactly the same as the one in Charlotte. I gave a soft chuckle and put my bag down.

A knock came at the door, and I went to answer it.

"This is for you, miss." The same receptionist was at the door, a small envelope in hand.

"Thanks," I said again and felt stupid, but she just nodded and left.

I took the envelope into the room and almost fell in the floor. There was $500 in the plain white paper! What was I supposed to do with this? I looked but there was no note, and the phone hadn't gone off. I'd been given a new SIM card for a nationwide phone service provider when I checked into the hotel in Charlotte, so I knew it wasn't a reception problem.

I stared at the money and decided to leave it alone for now. But… I took a single note out of the envelope and left my room. I wanted to see that bar. I didn't want to get drunk or anything like that; I just wanted to see where I'd be when I auditioned tomorrow. I followed signs on the wall that pointed to different parts of the hotel until I found the bar.

It was much bigger than I'd thought it would be. A stage was on the right side of the first floor. I wondered if they'd soundproofed the bar at all. I knew they must have, otherwise the noise would disturb hotel residents. I walked into the place, and a waitress with black hair, a black t-shirt with the name of the bar across her chest, and black jeans asked if I wanted a table or to sit at the bar.

"The bar, please," I told her and followed her to a seat.

The place was empty, and music played softly from the jukebox in one corner.

"What can I get you?" The bartender asked, a blond man with lovely gray eyes. Tall and muscular, he didn't look like the kind of man many would mess with, not with those broad shoulders and his height. He had to be over six and a half feet tall.

"Just a beer, please," I said and looked around. I'd seen the wink he gave me, but I let it go.

I looked over at the stage, saw the lights above that would spotlight the performers, and my heart thudded softly. I'd never really experienced stage fright, so I just closed my eyes and the world disappeared. I was actually quite excited to get up on that stage and perform. I wanted it desperately. I wanted it so much it surprised me.

"Thanks" I murmured as the beer appeared at my elbow, and the bartender walked away.

The room started to fill up as I sipped at the beer. There was room for a good crowd, and it would be a nice place for my first performance as a paid artist. If I got the gig.

I had to audition, but I was confident. The way people reacted to my music told me all I needed to know about my chances. Maybe it was a little bit of overconfidence, or stupidity, but I just knew I'd be on that stage more than once.

"How long has the bar been open?" I asked the bartender when he came my way to check on me.

"A couple weeks. They redesigned the whole thing; it was a jazz bar until then. Times have changed, and they decided to update it."

"So it was always a bar?"

I'd barely spoken to anyone for days now. It was nice to have someone to talk to.

"Yeah, but this is a new venture. We'll see how it goes." He excused himself when a man showed up with a request for drinks, and I turned in my bar stool to look around.

A good mix of younger patrons and old sat around in chairs, and a good crowd had built up. It would be a good venue and would keep money in the hotel. Not a bad idea.

It could have been worse. It could have been a lounge in an airport hotel. Or I could still be in London. I'd have to find a way to thank Kevin.

I saw a pen on top of the bar and picked it up to write lyrics on a napkin. The song flowed from the pen, and I had the music in mind already. I'd write it all down later and play it to make sure it all worked, but I knew I had a winner on my hands.

I kept pulling napkins from the dispenser on the bar and had a neat little stack by the time I paid my bill and left. I'd been given a chance many would die for, and tomorrow, I planned to make full use of it.

EMBER

Ember

"Next," I heard a voice call out and took a deep breath.

Beyond the curtain that hid the side of the stage sat three judges. People I didn't know, who would judge whether I suited their tastes or not. I had worked on the song all night, and it was perfect now. I bit my lips, tightened my grip on the guitar, and walked out to the stage.

I took a seat on the stool there and waited for their directions.

"Thanks. What do you have for us today?" A woman, blonde and beautiful, sat at one of the tables close to the stage with two men on each side of her. She had a smile on, but I'd been here as long as she had been. I knew the competition wasn't that fierce and couldn't help but feel even more confident.

I thought Kevin might be there, but he wasn't and that disappointed me a little, but I didn't let it stop me. "I have a self-composed song. It's called "Bad Habits.""

"Thanks, you can play when you're ready." The woman sat back, her gaze interested, but nothing more. There'd been seven performers before me. I knew she must have been bored by now.

I pushed down the number on my chest that a staff member had given me and brought up my guitar. I closed my eyes, strummed the guitar, and began to sing along to the music my fingers created. "You gave me the moon and took me through the stars. You took away my bad habits, but made me want more."

I saw three captivated faces when I opened my eyes for a moment and carried on through the next verse. By the time I'd finished I knew I had the gig. They hadn't been this animated all afternoon. All three clapped when I finished the song and the woman sat forward.

"What's your name, honey?" she asked, and I grinned.

"Ember Jones," I replied, and she looked like she'd just solved a puzzle.

"Right, you didn't need to audition. You're already on the list. But thank you for that. You just made the whole day worth it." I knew the competition behind me grumbled, but I didn't care.

"You're serious? I have the job?" I couldn't believe it, but at the same time, the impossible kept happening, so this wasn't that out of the ordinary.

"Yep. Says so right here." She held up a clipboard and grinned. "I'll see you later about the schedule."

"Oh my god. Thank you! Thank you so much!" I couldn't stop the way my hands shook as I stood up and walked off the stage.

A couple people congratulated me and told me I deserved it, but I didn't really hear it. All I could hear was the way my heart thudded in my chest as I walked off the stage. I'd just fulfilled a dream. A step on the road I'd wanted to travel for so long, but hadn't been able to step onto. Until now.

I took a deep breath and made my way to leave the bar, but a familiar face stopped my progress.

"What are you doing here?" I asked; it was the first question that popped to mind.

"Wow. You really are amazing," he replied and walked up to hug me.

"Kevin, seriously." I laughed, and returned the hug before quickly moving away. "Where have you been?"

"Taking care of some family stuff, but they can all fuck off for now. I wanted to see you. And talk to you. My brother has kept me way too busy, but I decided I'd had enough of it all."

"Oh." None of that really made sense to me, but I guess it did to him. "Did you do all of this?" I waved my hand around, and he smiled.

"I told you I could find you a job. This is the perfect one, don't you think? Did you get the contract?"

"What? No. I got an envelope with some money in it,

but I can't take all of that." I didn't want to give it back, but my pride wouldn't let me keep it all.

"Are you kidding? That's an advance on your pay! There was supposed to be a contract with it. I guess that got lost. Never mind, we'll sort that part later. Care to join me for dinner?"

"You want me to just go out to dinner with you now?" A sudden squeeze in my stomach made me feel sick as I realized he wanted something out of this after all.

"Well, yes. I thought you'd like some company."

"I'm not a prostitute you know?" I made to push past him when the realization that all of this was an expensive way to buy himself a woman dawned on me. "I would think a guy like you wouldn't have to buy a companion. Damn."

"What? No! Ember! Stop! What are you on about?"

"You're my sugar daddy is that it? I have to sleep with you for all of this? Well, I'd rather be on the street, thank you." I hated that my heart hurt so much, and I called myself a million kinds of fool. Of course, that was what he was after. Why else would a man go to so much trouble?

"Ember, no. You never have to sleep with me again if you don't want to. I have to admit, I rather enjoyed that night we shared together, but if you don't want that from me, then that's fine. It's a shame to waste that talent of yours, that's why I did this. I needed a singer, and you blew me away. I don't expect anything in return but for you to sign a contract with us and to hear that beautiful voice of yours for many nights to come."

I wanted his words to be true, and I studied his face to

find the lie, but I couldn't see one. "You… that's really all you want?"

"Yes! I wanted to celebrate and go over the contract with you, but you can say no to that too." His green eyes bored into mine, and I could tell he hadn't lied.

My stomach squeezed all over again when I remembered what those eyes looked like when he was over me, deep inside of me. I had to take in a quick breath to keep myself from going to him. I had to think about what he'd said. This wasn't about sex, but how much he wanted to help me. That was a good thing.

"Alright." Part of me wanted to believe him so badly that it almost frightened me. Men were dangerous. They could break your heart. Or your body. I'd learned to be careful, but so far Kevin had only shown me kindness.

And that smile of his was something I couldn't resist. The fullness of his bottom lip caught my attention, and I couldn't pull my gaze away.

When I'd seen him I'd wanted to rush to him, to throw myself in his arms, but I'd held myself back. I went to do that now and somehow tripped over a chair leg. I crashed into a waitress who had a tray full of freshly cleaned glasses and cringed when I heard them all shatter. Kevin caught me and asked if I was alright, but I brushed it all away.

"I'm fine, I'll pay for the glasses."

"Don't be silly; are you sure you're alright? What did you trip over?" He looked around, and I wondered if I should tell him now that I didn't have to trip over things, sometimes I was just clumsy like that. I knew he'd get used to it eventually, most people did who knew me.

"Where did you want to eat?" I asked to distract him and swung my case to walk out of the bar. It hit him in the back of the knee and he dropped like, well, like I'd hit him with my guitar case.

"Damn!" He groaned as he pushed himself up from the floor. "Sorry, I didn't realize I was in the way of your case."

"No, I'm sorry."

"No worries and no harm." He brushed himself off and grinned down at me. "Shall we drop that in your room before we go out?"

I felt desire spark inside of me the moment he said that. His eyes held mine, and I knew we both thought the same thing. An empty bedroom. His hand reached out for mine, and the mood changed.

He might have said I didn't have to sleep with him, but just then I wanted to. I wanted to so desperately. I'd just knocked over a dozen glasses and him, yet he was still there and hadn't said a word about my clumsiness.

And he was still as sexy as the moment I'd met him. I stepped closer, my heart a drum in my chest, and looked up into his eyes. "Kevin."

"Ember," he replied, and his arms came up to grip just below my shoulders. "I've wanted to see you since the moment I left you."

"I, I've been so alone..." I let the words trail off because I didn't know what I wanted to say, not really.

What could I say?

He pulled me closer, his lips so close. My eyes closed

but opened right back up as a shriek came from the stage. We pulled apart and looked in that direction. A new, ahem, performer, was on the stage and she'd started to sing. Scream. Whatever.

"Oh dear, that is…" I started to say but stopped when her scream went up a decibel or three.

"Fuck me, that's atrocious!" Kevin took my hand and pulled me away. We laughed as we walked swiftly away.

"That was a nightmare," I said as we waited for the elevator to take us up to the fifth floor.

"I knew you were the right choice." There was a weight to those words, and I looked up as the elevator doors opened.

"Thanks," I said and stepped into the small elevator. I thought he'd come in and stand beside me. Instead, he walked up to me until my head tilted back. He placed a hand on each side of my head and looked down at me.

"You can say no to me, Ember, whenever you want to. And I swear to you, I didn't do all of this to get a fuck out of you. I can get that in a million places. I did it for you. But damn, if I don't want to be inside of you again as you moan my name."

His lips cut off any response I might give and my arms went around his neck to pull him tighter to my face. Our tongues met, and something in my brain exploded with happiness. I hadn't let myself dare hope he'd want me like this again, and part of me had been afraid that was all he wanted, but I knew that wasn't the situation. And I wanted him, I'd wanted him from the moment he'd walked into the bar; even when I almost walked away from him, I'd wanted him.

"The elevator doors will open in a moment," he said, his lips still wet from my kiss. His eyes had turned a darker shade, almost a brown color as he'd kissed me, and now they were directly on mine. "Do you want me to follow you to your room, or should I hold the doors while you drop off your case?"

I swallowed hard around a lump in my throat and told my tongue to work for something other than swirling around his. *Use your words, Ember.*

"Uh..." The door dinged as we came to a stop. My eyes darted behind us, then back to his. "I want..."

"Hurry, before the doors shut." His fingers traced down my jaw, and I couldn't look away.

"Come in with me. Please."

It might be a mistake, it might lead to more hurt, but my body remembered his touch; the way he felt against me, inside of me, and I couldn't say no.

Kevin took my hand and pulled us out just before the doors shut again. I used my key card to let us in and walked to my bedroom. "Do you want a drink?"

"I only want you, Ember," he said as he pushed me down gently to the bed.

I stared up at him, this real man who stood over me with a hot look in his eyes. I hummed, but it wasn't a word, or even an attempt at a word; it was just a reaction to that look. Oh boy. He leaned over me, his hands to either side of my head, and brought his face down to mine.

Heat, wet, then the sensual sensation of his tongue as it

slid over mine. My hands came up to pull him down, and he settled between my thighs.

"Kevin…" I whispered his name against his lips as he pressed into me, hard and ready.

"I promised myself I'd give you time. I'd let you settle in before I let this go any further. But I can't. I want you too much. I've never wanted anyone the way I want you." His lips brushed along my jaw to whisper into my ear, "I can't say no to you. Why is that?"

"I don't know," I flubbed, too caught up in the way his lips brushed at the place beneath my earlobe. Who knew how fantastic that was?

My fingers tightened on his shoulders, and my hips pushed up into his. "Why do you fascinate me like you do?"

He pressed back into the push of my hips, and we both groaned. It felt too good. "I don't know, but I couldn't stop thinking about you either."

"That's good," he said with a raised eyebrow. His voice had gone deeper, quieter just before his lips brushed against mine again.

"I need…" I started, but couldn't finish. I needed so much, and he'd given me far too much already.

"You can have it all, Ember. Whatever you want." He began to move, and his hands pulled at my shirt until it was gone and all I had on was my bra and jeans. I'd kicked off my shoes the minute I walked into the room, as had he. "All you have to do is ask."

"I want you to fuck me, Kevin. I want you to make me turn inside out, like you did before." To me the words were bold and showed just how far I'd come. I didn't think I'd ever spoken so boldly about anything I'd wanted before. Nothing.

"I can give you exactly what you need, Ember." His hand came up to grip firmly at my breast. His thumb slid over the nipple, and I felt a spark that burned all the way down to where our bodies met.

I let my head fall back against the pillows and sighed in a breath of air. I knew from experience I'd need all the air I could get.

9

EMBER

Ember

Kevin kissed my neck, and I felt the brush of silky strands of hair as he moved them away with his lips.

"More..." I forgot the rest of what I wanted to say as my pulse jumped and heat surged through my veins. I pressed up into him again as he put his arms around me to pull me tight to his body while his other hand cupped the full globe of one of my breasts. He'd focused on me, his face a fierce mask of concentration, and I didn't want to interrupt him.

I pressed my hips against him and pushed my breast into his hand. He could make me feel like a woman, he could make me feel like I mattered, just with a single stroke of his finger. This was almost more than I could handle, but I knew I could take this and a whole lot more.

I let him touch me, soothe away my fears with his fingers and lips, his body a solace I hadn't known I needed.

I probably should have told him to wait for me, but I knew, I just knew, this was right. It wasn't even a question anymore. The world had kicked me far too often not to take the pieces of joy that came my way now. This might not be love, but surely it was more than just a fuck?

I stopped caring when his lips pushed away the lace of my bra and took my nipple into heat that made my hips move to their own rhythm. Each brush of my body against his sparked a gasp from me, and pleasure was already within reach; it came with each stroke of his body against mine.

I didn't think he'd have to get my clothes off before I was a wreck in his arms. He paused his suction on my nipple long enough to make a noise to soothe me, before he started it all over again. Frantic, my body was frantic with the need to find that place again; it *needed* that place, and only Kevin could give it to me.

His fingers slid down between us, to grasp at my ass through my jeans. The sensation set off new sparks, in an area I didn't know could stir pleasure or so much fucking anticipation.

"Kevin. Fuck. What is that?" I moaned the words, not sure if I really expected or wanted an answer. I knew it felt good, and in the end I didn't care why.

It seemed he didn't want to pause long to answer; instead, his tongue flicked at my nipple as he sucked it harder, and I hissed in a breath.

I pushed at his shoulders. I wanted to come with him

inside of me, but my legs wrapped around his hips to hold him tightly to me. I wasn't sure what I wanted right now, but Kevin knew exactly what to give me.

I gasped again when his fingers curled around my ass to tilt my hips deeper into his. My body throbbed, it pulsed with the ache of pleasure he gave me. Every part of me buzzed, and he knew it. By the time that hand slid into my pants and curled around to find my wet center, I was on the edge. A warm, slick finger slid into me gently. Only a little, enough to know it was there. And then it slid in deeper, and I held my breath. Any minute now. I groaned as he went deeper, and my hips pressed into him, to take all of that finger. My hands clutched at his shoulders in anticipation.

His palm pressed into my ass, while his finger dipped in and out of me, his tongue a flickering bee against my nipple. And that was it. I was over the edge that only he'd ever pushed me over.

I wanted to fuck him. I didn't want this to be the end of it, and I knew it wouldn't be. Kevin was a focused man, and right now, I was all he focused on. Making me come was his goal, and he had reached that with determined patience.

I ground into his hand, shocked at how good it felt to have his palm pressed into my ass, but not willing to let it go. It felt too good, he felt too good.

I wanted what he was going to give me in just a minute, and that anticipation, that knowledge, let me enjoy this moment.

I'd only just begun to come down when he pulled away

long enough to strip us of our clothes that remained. He threw them over his shoulders and was back between my thighs before I could blink. I moved my legs, opened my body to him, and felt the intrusion of his cock as he pushed into me.

"Fuck," he gasped out as he sank into me, and all I could do was clutch at his shoulders. I felt him pause as a shudder passed through him before he adjusted his hands and then pulled my hips tight to his while he sank to his knees.

He began a steady pace, a slow grind while he listened for the thrust that made me gasp in just the right way. When he heard that sound and the quickness of my breath picked up, he spoke.

"I'm going to fuck you until we both come, Ember. Later on, I'm going to explore every inch of you all over again, but for now, I'm going to fuck you until we come apart. Can you get a finger on that sweet little clit of yours? I want to feel your hand between us as I slam into you." He kept fucking me, but he gave a nod when he felt my hand move. "That's it, baby girl, make yourself come all over me."

I found the spot he wanted me to touch, but I wasn't sure I needed to; I was already too close. The way he moved inside of me, the way he talked to me, was all I needed. He slid deeper into me, and I never wanted it to end. It was too much, it wasn't enough, but his lips on my neck soothed me, kept me right there with him.

Kevin had kept us at a slow pace, but when I hitched in a breath of air he began to move faster, deeper, and I didn't have to ask for anything, because he'd already done it. I could feel the moment was near, and I forgot to breathe as something within me bloomed into a wave that I couldn't escape. Good thing I didn't want to.

I couldn't speak then. I could only strangle out a sound, an indication that I was lost, but didn't care. Kevin kept moving, kept driving into me, as I grasped at the bedsheets to hold on. I might explode into a million pieces otherwise. His satisfied chuckle didn't stop me either; I just rode the wave he'd pushed me into.

It was then that he followed me, when I'd stopped breathing, when all of my sounds stopped, and I was in that magical place of nothing. He joined me there, and that was it.

When it was done and we'd both stopped shuddering, he rolled down beside me, but pulled me close to his body. "I've missed you."

I wanted to say, *how could you miss me, you barely know me,* but didn't. I just curled into him, my leg over his hips. "I didn't think I'd see you again."

"What? Why? After all of this?" His head turned to look down at me where I had my head on his chest. "It's not my usual style, I have to admit, but you're different, Ember. You're just…"

I swear his cheeks turned red, but that might have been from our previous exertion. He looked away for a moment and then turned back to me. "You're something special, Ember. Maybe one day you'll realize that. You've only ever needed someone to believe in you, and well, I'm happy to be that person for you now."

"Thank you." What else could I say? It was my turn to

look away, even though that didn't stop the flush of pleasure that burned through me. Now, I was the one doing the blushing.

"Come on, let's shower and then go out. I want to show you Nashville, take you to dinner, and talk about the future with you." He pulled me tight for a moment before he dropped a kiss on the top of my head. "I want to just be with you, if that's okay?"

"That's well." I couldn't think of what to say; I was too pleased to say much of anything, really. "That's fine."

We managed to get through a shower without too much distraction, although he did back me against the wall to kiss me senseless at one point before he ducked my head under the showerhead to wash my hair. I could only laugh and let him have his way. After we dried off and dressed, he realized I still had on the clothes I'd worn in London.

"You haven't got more clothes yet?" he asked, and I looked down at the floor.

"I didn't have any money to get new ones." I thought about the money in the envelope. "I got the money in the envelope, but I didn't know what it was for, and didn't want to spend too much of it."

"You're a smart girl, Ember." His narrowed eyes looked at me for a moment before he grinned. "Alright, let's get you some clothes first then. That was your advance by the way."

"Ah, right, you did say." I smiled, put my arm in his, and followed him out of the door.

He then took me to several shops where we bought outfits he called my stage costumes, and I could only gape at him. Long dramatic dresses fit for a rockabilly queen, black leather pants and colorful silk tops, boots, and other things I couldn't imagine wearing, but he said it would be important as I created a style. I protested the cost of all of the clothes, but he said they'd go on the company account as part of my contract. Then he bought me clothes to wear every day. It was a small fortune, but he wouldn't let me say no.

The trunk of the very expensive white car he'd driven us around in was full by the time we headed to a restaurant to eat. I couldn't believe it was all for me; he'd even found some costume jewelry for me to wear. That sensation of being asleep while awake came back, and I went quiet while I waited for reality to set in.

"You deserve this, Ember, you know that don't you?" His hand came to cover mine across the table the waiter had brought us to.

"I don't know, Kevin. Is this all a really long dream? Am I in a coma somewhere? This isn't how my life is supposed to be." I hadn't told him a whole lot about my past, but I was sure I'd given enough away by now for him to know what my life had been like before I met him.

"It's real, Ember. Every second of it is real. Fate decided I needed to meet you and give you this chance. Why do you think you don't deserve it?" His green eyes were confused, but I could see amusement there too. It pleased him that I was so shocked still. That didn't bother me. Sometimes people took great delight in helping others, and Kevin had done far more than that. He'd given me a whole new life.

"So what's this contract about?" I lifted brown eyes to

his and held my breath as he ticked off the main points of the contract.

"For now, it's only for a season, but if you want to continue with us, we'll extend it to a year. This is your pay for that time period." He wrote down a number on a napkin that made my eyes water. "And, of course, your expenses will be covered: new strings for your guitar, travel costs if you go to one of our other hotels, and food will be the kinds of things we'll cover for you."

He listed off more things, and I knew this couldn't be normal. He had taken a special interest in me and my career. I couldn't say no, I had to admit. This was the chance of a lifetime.

"And no, you are not obligated to have sex with me ever again. Although, I would like to take you to the back of this restaurant and find a nice, quiet spot to fuck you in." Those last words were spoken low, and I had to lean in to hear them.

I grinned, and my eyes went wide with shock as his words had an effect on me. "Right here?"

I'd whispered the words, but he heard me. "Oh yes, right here, Ember."

"But there's so many people…" I looked around and felt the flush start to rise in my chest to my cheeks. "Wouldn't they hear us?"

"Possibly, but it wouldn't matter. For now, I can wait." His eyes contained a heat I knew he wanted to unleash, but he held it back. "I can't promise that will be true by the time we're finished with our meals."

I looked down at the place where our hands met and

smiled. This man had given me an entirely new world in so many ways. Now he wanted to show how much he wanted me. No man had ever done that. I'd been a tool to the first man who had me; now, I had one who wanted to give to me and not use. The world was my oyster at that moment, and Kevin had given all of that to me. Somewhere in my chest, a lock I hadn't realized was on my heart turned and began to open.

10

—

EMBER

Ember

I went over the list of songs I had planned for my first night on the stage and took a deep breath. I'd had a week to rehearse, to work with the band the hotel had hired for me, and now it was only hours away. The breath calmed me down, and I felt my confidence rise.

In my normal life I was a very quiet person. I tended to stay in the background so I wouldn't be noticed. That had worked to keep me out of trouble and out of the spotlight, most of the time. That suited me. I wasn't an overly confident person, except for those moments when I held my guitar. I knew I could tell a story, that I could evoke emotions in my audience, not just within myself, and that really boosted me.

The people who managed the bar had asked if I planned

to do covers or if I had my own music. I'd told them I'd play my own music, and they'd asked to hear it. Kevin sat in the audience as I played the songs he and I had chosen. I'd played them for him one day in the apartment assigned to me by the hotel. The managers had chosen the songs they liked the best, and I'd worked with the band to add drums, a fiddle, and another guitar.

I'd never had a band before, I hadn't been brave enough to approach other people to ask if they would play with me, but the people in the band seemed to get my sound and quickly came up with music to accompany me with. Now, it was the big day, and I was a little nervous.

My palms were sweaty, and I kept wiping them on the black leather pants I had on. Paired with an elbow-length top that Jackson Pollack would adore, with splotches of every color in the rainbow on a white background, I looked the part. My hair was in its naturally curly state, and a makeup artist had taught me how to apply stage makeup. I was as ready as I could be.

The bar had reservations for tables already, and every seat would be full. No pressure, right? I looked at myself in the bathroom mirror in the hotel and took another deep breath. Should I eat before or after? I didn't want a rumble from my tummy to interrupt my set and make the crowd laugh.

Maybe some chips or a bit of toast? I headed into the kitchen and looked around. I'd become used to the place over the last few days and now it seemed like home. It was mine, and I'd started to leave little bits of me around the place. A notebook I wrote songs in was on the coffee table.

A picture I'd found in a shop and couldn't live without, a drawing of a ballerina in a pose was on the wall instead of the generic picture of orchids that had hung there before. The kitchen now had a brand of coffee I'd adored from the first taste in a canister on the counter. A set of lime green glasses sat in the dish drain, another purchase I'd made.

A coverlet I'd bought because I adored the old-style quilted pattern was folded over a kitchen chair, and I picked it up to take back to the couch. And my wine. A box of muscadine wine sat on the counter. A dark, sweet red wine that looked absolutely amazing in the tall wine glasses I'd bought.

When I was a child we'd used empty jelly jars as glasses and butter tubs as bowls. With Graham, we'd done the same, even when he had won a lot of money from a poker game. That made me pause, and I stopped to think. Maybe he was dealing drugs even back then? The man wasn't the most patient guy in the world, and I'd learned to tell when he was lying after a stupid amount of time. Could he sit through a poker game without giving himself away?

"Huh. I bet he was dealing drugs back then. That bastard!" I didn't always swear out loud, but the moment deserved it.

Even when Graham had a lot of money in his pockets, we'd lived in a hovel, until we couldn't afford even that. When he'd come home with a lot of money and said we were going to England, I'd wanted to get away from the poverty I'd known all of my life. I'd jumped at the chance, basically.

I'd had a feeling that trip was planned as a drug run

from day one. I remembered now the way Graham had messed with my guitar case, and how he'd insisted on carrying it from the airport. He'd helped the driver put it in the back of our taxi when we got there, and now I could remember how he'd messed with the case again when we got to the hotel. Had he used my case to carry it all in?

Heat from my anger made my cheeks burn red, but I couldn't help it. That… twat! Only, I thought it in the way the English had said it, as if they were saying cat instead of the way we say it in America, which sounded more like hot. That fucking twat!

It wasn't all bad though. That decision to follow the man I'd thought I'd loved across the pond had led to this moment. A moment when people would listen to me sing, hear my songs, my stories. I wanted to dance I was so happy.

Only, I couldn't dance. I had two left feet, obviously, so I'd never learned to dance properly. It was one of the reasons I would play from a bar stool tonight; I just had to hope I wouldn't fall off of it. Maybe a chair would be better?

I pondered the choice as I walked into the bedroom and sat down on my bed. I sent Kevin a message and asked what he thought. He had some work to do and had left my place early this morning. Sometimes, when he was at work, he could be a little impatient, or even cold, but he always made up for it with a kiss when he came back to me.

His brothers had left him alone, but I always knew when they called him or sent him a text message. He'd go tense, growl, and prowl off to stand on the balcony of my room while he talked to them. He didn't seem to care for his brothers very much. Especially the one named Trent. He was closer to the one called Mason, but he still went stiff when it was Mason who wanted his attention.

He'd told me about his family, and how he adored his sister, but his father had always pitted the boys against each other. It didn't help that Trent seemed to think he was the king of the roost, but I didn't give my opinion on it all. It seemed dysfunction struck even the rich. I'd always thought it was a symptom of poverty, but I could see it wasn't now.

We'd had a week of bliss so far, and I'd come to learn some of his quirks. When his brothers needed his attention he could be distant, and I didn't like that, but I didn't push. Our relationship was still too new. I didn't want to intrude or upset him. One day, I'd ask him more about his family.

I'd told him about my past one very long night and how I'd grown up. He'd been amazed at how I'd managed to survive childhood with drug addicts for parents. He didn't chide me when I told him I hadn't gone back to check on my mother. She'd forgotten about me the moment Graham came along. She'd seen him as the new dummy who had me as a burden. Her addiction had become worse after that, and I stopped trying to help her. She didn't want my help.

It was a cold decision, but one she'd taught me to make. If the bird wouldn't fly, why try to force it? I hadn't given up on her; she had, a long time ago. I couldn't sit around and watch her self-destruct, and I'd left her in my past. It was all a kid could do, right?

Maybe I wasn't the best person in the world, but there was nothing else I could have done. Mom wanted her drugs far more than me and always had. I couldn't change that. I'd been an accident, a night of sex, drugs, and rock and roll gone wrong, and she didn't want me. It was a miracle I hadn't been born addicted to the drugs she'd taken, but she'd stopped in the late stages of her pregnancy because she'd been living with my grandmother then. Grams had promised to raise me, if Mom would just lay off the drugs and give me a chance.

The problem was, Grams had passed away before I could leave the nest on my own. I'd lost her guidance and her strength, and it had nearly broken me. When I'd been taken to my mother's, ahem, home, I'd wanted to run back to my grandmother's house. It had only been a rental though, and my mother had already cleared it out before my grandmother had even been buried.

I'd felt alone from that moment on. Graham had relieved that loneliness for a little while, but as time had gone by, it had started to creep back into my life. Until the day he kicked me out. I still didn't want to think about that night. The cold, the fear, it was too much to deal with. I'd hunted for a homeless shelter of any kind, but couldn't find one and had found the building after hours of walking. I'd gone in afraid, terribly afraid, but it had gotten me out of the wet, cold snow that fell from the sky, and I'd huddled in the darkness there until the sun came up.

The situation could have been much worse, I knew that. Kevin had saved me in so many ways. I was grateful to him for that, but gratitude wasn't all that drove our relationship. It wasn't just the sex either, although that was good.

The man knew how to touch a woman, just the right way to drive the desired response, and I think that had given me a confidence that I'd never had before. He made me feel beautiful, even when his hand slid over the bulge around my hips that would disappear if I'd lay off the chips. His hands cupped my breasts and found their soft weight amazing, not overly ripe. He never criticized me, or my weight, and he told me more than once that I was beautiful.

He respected me, and he showed me that all the time. I loved his kindness, the way he treated me, although he could sometimes be a snob. I laughed now at the way he'd cringed when a waiter had brought him the wrong fork for his dinner one night. *One does not eat fish with a normal knife and fork,* he'd sneered. I'd had to look away or burst out laughing at him.

I bet he ate spaghetti with a fork and spoon too, I thought now, and sat down on the couch. I was falling in love with the man, and there was little I could do about it. I didn't want to do anything about it, if I was honest. He might have been a little snobby, and sometimes he was distant, but he was also gentle, caring, and generous. Not just to me either. I'd seen the tips he'd given to people, and heard how he'd instructed the manager to give the waitress who had fallen at home and broken her ankle her wages, whether she came in or not. Money wasn't something to be hoarded, according to Kevin.

It was meant to be used, enjoyed, and shared. I'd got the

impression over the last few days that his older brother, Trent, was a hoarder, while Mason was a spender. The other two brothers seemed selfish, whereas Kevin wasn't at all. Not that I'd seen anyway.

I looked up at the clock on the wall of the kitchen and realized it was time to go downstairs and face the music. Play the music, one of those. It had sunk in that I was about to play to an audience, and I had to really impress. Kevin deserved that I go beyond my best after all he'd done for me. I had to repay that somehow, because he'd already said he wouldn't take payment for anything that he'd done.

My phone vibrated as I took the elevator down, and I pulled it out of my back pocket to look at it. A message from Kevin. "I'll see you soon. I know you'll blow everyone away."

There was a kiss emoji, and that made me smile. I had a feeling Kevin Thompson had never sent an emoji in his life before I came along. He was an odd character, American in so many ways, but with a hint of the British reserve I'd become accustomed to in my time over there. It made me smile. He was trying his best.

He'd said he'd never really been in a relationship before, not one like ours, and that meant a lot to me. Alright, our relationship was still brand new, but I felt as if I already knew the man. I knew he hated to wake up to an alarm clock, but often had to. I knew he loved orange juice with his breakfast. That he wanted to find a way to end poverty across the globe, and that he often thought in terms of the global community, rather than on a micro level.

In many ways, Kevin went beyond his reserve, his

private-school background, and used what he'd learned to help others. He had even started a foundation for that change, although it was still in the early stages of development. It was nice to know he had some brains behind all of that money and privilege. More importantly, Kevin had the heart to go with those brains, and that was amazing to me.

I walked through the bar, to the back of the stage, and sat down as a woman came at me with a powder puff and the snap of chewing gum. "You ready, sugar?"

I wanted to laugh at the country twang that escaped Elmira's mouth, but didn't. Mine wasn't much better. "I'm as ready as I'll ever be, Elmira. I just hope I don't forget the words."

"That's something weird you singers have. You wrote the songs, how can you forget the words?" Her gum snapped as she gave me one last pat, and I looked up at her with amused eyes.

"I don't know, but if I find out, I'll tell you."

She gripped my hands, popped her gum once more, and grinned down at me. "You got this, sugar. I've heard you in your rehearsals. You got this and then some."

I took a deep breath and gnawed at my lip as I stared at the door. It was almost showtime.

11

KEVIN

Kevin

I glared at my phone as Mason's voice droned through the speaker. Would he never shut up? I'd had it from Trent earlier, and now Mason.

"Are you sure about this woman, Kevin?" Mason asked. Trent had asked the same thing.

"I'll video it all for you, live stream it on YouTube or something. But yes, she's worth it." I'd never had to defend myself like this. Why now?

A little voice deep down said it was because I'd never shown so much interest in a single woman before. I'd had a few dates with some, sex with plenty, but I'd never spent so much money, or made so much effort for one woman before.

"Well, you know Trent is going to hold you personally

responsible for all of this, right? If she crashes and burns, so do you." Mason's voice now sounded as if he didn't care what happened, but something drove him to act anyway.

"What's got up your nose, Mason? Why do you care about the family business all of a sudden? Don't you have a party to go to or something?" I thought it would shut him up, but it didn't.

"Oh, if you hadn't run off to Tennessee you'd know why. Trent's basically dumped everything in my lap to teach us both a lesson. You and me. But you're handling things there, so I guess I shouldn't blame you."

"We could always call in Emily, you know?" I offered, but knew it was pointless and Mason knew it too.

"She's too busy with Dad. Whatever game he's playing, she's involved with it. Bless her, she only ever wants to please him. To her own detriment." Mason sighed down the line, and I knew there was more on his mind than business.

"What's up, brother? What's got you twisted up?" We didn't usually have heart to heart talks, but I could tell something was wrong.

"Nothing. Just this woman I met."

"Ah…" I quickly interrupted. "So you know where I'm at do you?"

"Has she got your brain spinning and your guts twisted up in knots?" Mason groaned down the line.

"She has indeed, Mason. I can't think about much else except Ember."

"That's where I'm at right now. A total mess trying to figure out this business shit I never wanted to be involved in anyway." Mason sighed, and I could hear him shift on the other end of the phone. "Well, I wish you both luck. You'll need it if she flops."

"She won't. I know she won't. She'll have them all eating out of her hand in seconds flat." That wasn't a lie, I knew she would, I'd seen it in England. Not everyone had stopped, but the ones who did were transfixed.

Ember was beautiful, there was no doubt of that, even if she wasn't the model type. She was beautiful and that voice combined with her beauty would draw a person in. Her songs were good, really good, and I knew she could make this work.

I wanted to see her before the show started, but she'd said she didn't want that. She needed to do this her way, for now. Later, when she got used to it, I was sure she'd be fine, but for now, she wanted seclusion and quiet before she started.

"I've got to go, Mason. She'll be starting soon and I have to find Mark and Paula, the managers of the bar. I'll send you a notification when I start recording." I waited for him to say goodbye and then I went to my desk in the office. A few papers to sign, a purchase order that needed review, a few other things, but they could wait. I needed to be down there when she started. Even if she couldn't see me in the crowd.

Mark and Paula had saved seats for us at the back of the bar so that paying customers could sit up front. I heard the hum of a crowd as I walked toward the bar and smiled. We had a good crowd then, even if none of them had ever heard of Ember. This was our first attempt at a musical event since we'd remodeled the bar. Ember would bring in thousands more over the next few months, I just knew it.

"Hey, Kevin, over here," Paula called out, and I went to the table. Paula was a beautiful woman, with dark hair and darker eyes, but I wasn't interested. I only had eyes for Ember, even if Paula had made it obvious more than once that she wouldn't turn me down.

Maybe in the past I'd have taken her up on the offer, but not anymore. I didn't want anyone else. It was that simple.

"Hey, guys. How are you?" I sat down, gave the waitress my order for a scotch, and looked around.

There was a buzz in the air from the crowd and an excitement that grew as the drinks started to flow. People ordered snacks to go with their drinks, and I could see a sea of happy faces as the time passed.

"I think she's going to be fine," Mark said, and I turned to him.

"Yeah, I think she'll be fine too. She's never played in front of a crowd like this before, but I don't think she'll let us down. She was born for this moment."

"She's definitely got the talent, but then again, a lot do in this town," Paula said, and I turned my gaze to her. "Singers are a dime a dozen here, but Ember…"

I waited because she was within an inch of being fired. If she didn't believe in the woman we'd hired to sing for us, then I couldn't trust her decisions.

"Ember gives me chills," Paula finished and I relaxed.

"She's done that to me a time or two, as well." I sipped at the scotch the waitress brought me and put the glass down.

I knew the list Ember planned to play over the next hour. It was a good list, I'd heard every single song, and knew they were perfect. Some sad, some happy, and one was just downright... badass. Exactly what she'd portray on that stage tonight.

A badass woman who didn't need anyone.

I took a breath and let it out through dry lips. I was nervous, but it was more about my reaction to the situation than anything to do with Ember. I was nervous for her. Not because I thought she'd fail, but because I knew people could be dicks.

I had faith though. This night would be magical, I just knew it. I settled back in my chair and waited with everybody else.

We didn't have to wait for long. The lights went down and the crowd went quiet as the spotlight moved to highlight Ember alone on the stage.

"Hey there, everybody. I'm Ember, and I'm going to sing a few songs for you tonight. I've written all of them, and each one has a special meaning to me. I hope they stir a memory for you and make you smile."

"That's my girl," I said softly, my hand clenched. She didn't look afraid or nervous, just her normal calm self.

Until she went to sit down on the bar stool. She didn't quite manage it the first time, but laughed it off with a joke to the crowd. That put them at ease and helped them connect with her. *That's it, baby, play it cool.*

She strummed her fingers over the guitar strings. There'd been a few titters and loud laughs, but as soon as she opened her mouth and began to sing, the crowd went still and quiet. Her voice was clear as she sang, her eyes closed most of the time, but they'd open to connect with someone in the crowd. She'd smile and close her eyes again.

There was so much emotion in each verse, every word was a compliment to the next, and the pace of the song was just right. Ember had fans from that moment on. When the lights dimmed for a second and then came back on with her band in place, the crowd cheered.

"This is a song I wrote recently. I was in a tough spot, and a very special man came along and saved me. I can never thank him enough for what he did for me, so I wrote this song for him. Thank you, Kevin. I know you're out there." She put her hand over her eyes as a screen and looked out. "Somewhere."

The crowd laughed again, and I knew she was a totally different woman on the stage from the woman I'd met in a park in London. This woman was confident, self-assured and ready to take on the world. I was breathless as I watched her.

The song was beautiful, and as she sang about the moon and the stars and how she now owned a few stars to keep as her own, because I'd given them to her, I felt something inside me change. It had been a lonely, empty place, but now it was full of Ember. I thought I really, truly fell in love with her in that moment. As the song ended the crowd stood and cheered. They wanted to hear it again, demanded to hear it again, and Ember gave them what they wanted with a chuckle.

The second rendition was just as soul-stirring as the

first and when it ended, I could see tears in her eyes as the crowd almost screamed the house down. Yeah, she was going to be a hit. Was a hit. We had to find a way to get her music out there.

"Call Jerry over at the recording studio. You know, the guy who comes in sometimes?" I waited for Mark to acknowledge he knew who I was on about and continued, "Get her in the studio as soon as possible."

I'd known she was a gem before, but now I knew the crowd would know it. Already the pings on my phone were getting out of control. I'd set it up on a tripod on the table and had recorded from the moment she came out on the stage. I could see that there'd already been over 500 likes on the live stream. People were subscribing to the channel and leaving messages.

"Who is this goddess?" I saw one commenter post.

"Oh my god, I want to have her babies," a female commenter replied, and that made me laugh. Ember had gone off the stage for a moment to have a break, but would be back in a few minutes. I almost ran backstage to show her the success she'd already had, but thought I should wait. I didn't want to jinx her performance.

My phone continued to ping, even during the break, and I looked at the others at the table and laughed. "If we don't get her in a recording contract soon, somebody else will."

It was one of the plans of the chain and one of the reasons we were in Nashville. We wanted to start a recording label, and with Ember as our first artist, I thought we'd be a hit.

"I would have to agree, Kevin. I kind of knew it before, but I wanted to be sure she could handle the stage and a crowd," Mark said, and Paula nodded.

"She's going to destroy the charts with those songs. Nobody else will be able to get on them."

It was only when a commenter agreed with us that I realized the camera was picking up our conversation. I laughed and typed a reply. That got a slew of posts, and I knew I'd have to hire someone else to manage our social media pages. This was getting out of hand. I laughed, and the other two came over to see what had me going.

My phone, now a camera for the moment, was buzzing in the tripod every time someone liked, subscribed, or left a message. The viewers loved it and they were bringing their friends in.

"What's all the fuss about?" one commenter asked, and about twenty more responded with, "Wait for it."

Ember soon came back to the stage to a large round of applause and began to play again. The fiddler joined in, and then the drums. It was just enough to give the song a kick, and I decided the band behind her had to be the ones to play with Ember. They'd all meshed together perfectly, and every instrument brought something evocative to the song.

"Book them too," I told Mark, and the commenters on my phone agreed. I laughed and went back to watching the woman I'd finally realized I loved.

She might forget me once she was a superstar. That thought came out of nowhere to torment me. I decided I'd just have to be the man she needed me to be. That was all I could do. As long as she was happy with the world, that was all I cared about.

I watched for the rest of her set and waited until the moment when I could go back to her. I wanted to protect her from the world, but at the same time, I wanted to give her to the world. It was an odd road to be on, but it was the one I'd chosen for myself the moment I heard her sweet voice in the park. She deserved whatever the world could give her. I'd just given the world a star, I knew it deep in my bones.

Now, I just had to protect her from it. There were a lot of cheats in this business, people who would take advantage of her and throw her away once they'd wrung every dime they could out of her. I didn't want that. I wanted to give her everything instead.

And as she sang her last song, a song about finding love at last, I knew she was the one. That one. The final and best one. The woman I'd spend the rest of my life with. It didn't bother me a bit. I'd suspected it from the start, but knew it for sure now. Ember was the woman of my dreams, and the one I'd spend the rest of my life with.

12

———

EMBER

Ember

"I'm busy tomorrow, can we make it sometime next week?" My head was turned down to hear my phone against my shoulder as I typed into my laptop.

I'd bought it with my earnings two months ago. I could afford it now, especially when Kevin increased my pay every single week. It had been almost three months since that first awesome night on the stage, and I barely had a moment of peace anymore.

I was on the phone with a local radio host now who wanted to interview me. I had a lot of requests for that now. I also had a lot of managers, agents, and producers knocking on the door to my dressing room. I turned them all down. I wasn't ready for that yet, but the interviews would help the bar. Those I went on.

I'd gone from filling the bar with patrons of the hotel to having a crowd of people from the area coming in too. They'd had to add more seats as word of my songs spread around town. I was sure a lot of people were talented in this town, it was one of the main reasons it existed, after all, but everybody said there was something special about me.

I could barely take it all in, but tried my best to. At times, Kevin would disappear, but it was business, and he'd always come back, hungrier for me than ever. Those were the nights he got really wild and blew my mind.

I couldn't help but grin as I brushed a stray lock of hair out of my face. I had it clipped up in a messy knot on my head and had on a simple zip up bathrobe of dark blue terrycloth. I looked terrible, but I knew if Kevin walked in the door right now, he'd still think I was the most beautiful woman on earth.

Except for the infrequent disappearing acts he'd pull, everything was perfect. I didn't have anything to worry about, and life was grand. I'd never been happier, and I didn't want to scratch at the surface too much. Less than three months wasn't very long, and I'd decided to let the relationship develop as it wanted to. I didn't push for declarations of love or make plans for the future. I just lived for the day, and today, I had decided to have some downtime before my set this evening.

I'd been going non-stop all this time, with only a day or two off when I had to have one. I was working hard to reach my goals, and right now, my goal was to give my all to the contract that would be up soon. We hadn't discussed what came next, but I knew Kevin had plans for my future. If his brothers would stop bugging him all the time, we might find time to talk about the future. In between sex.

That made me giggle more than I should have. I wanted to make an album, something that was solid and that I could hold in my hands. The bar had a YouTube site, and my songs were already making us all money, but I wanted more. I wanted a real contract and to go on tour. In the future. I wasn't in a huge rush. I wanted to make sure Kevin was paid back what I owed him, and I knew he wanted to be part of my future, but I was getting antsy. Those trips away.

He wouldn't call me while he was away. He'd said often that he was too busy to think most of the time much less to call me, and when he walked out of the office he was too exhausted. That was why he was so desperate for me when he came back. That made me feel good, that he wanted me so much, but it didn't really help me when I wanted to talk to him about important things.

I could feel my face droop, and I went to pour myself a glass of wine. It was a dessert wine, so I wouldn't get tipsy until the second glass. *Depending how much I filled the glass,* I thought with a snicker. I had a feeling I'd be alone until it was time to go downstairs, so I could have a nap before I showered and went down anyway. One glass wouldn't be a problem.

I scrolled through the website that had been set up for me and saw the page visits had increased. A lot. My name was spreading, and that started a warm glow in my chest. People had started to notice me. That wasn't a bad thing.

I'd never let myself dream before, but now I'd been given permission to do just that. I had started to dream big, but only Kevin knew that. Only Kevin knew my innermost thoughts.

He knew I wanted to go back to England, to perform there, in the place where I'd finally been noticed. Where I'd been at the lowest point in my life before one incredible man changed it all. He knew I wanted to sing at festivals, at bars, on a stage, as the main act. He knew all of that.

But not a single other person did or would. Those were my secrets. I knew he'd keep them.

I hummed as I flipped from the website to my Facebook page. I had a lot of friend invites from people I didn't know, messages from men who wanted to give me babies, and fans who really wanted to connect. It was strange what some people would do online, I'd come to find out. Luckily, this wasn't my personal page, and I allowed most of the people who'd sent requests. I'd weed out the bad ones over time.

I hummed an old song under my breath as I sipped at my wine and went to my Twitter feed, also a public account, not my private one. A lot of new people there, and a whole lot of tweets about how much people had enjoyed my shows and the hotel. Alright, good marketing for both of us. I smiled happily and wished Kevin were here. I really missed him when he was gone, and couldn't wait for him to get back.

My phone buzzed, and I saw it was one of the women who acted as a bartender downstairs. They'd had to hire another one to keep up, and she and I clicked really well. "What's up, girl?"

"Honey, you wouldn't believe what just walked in down here. A load of women from the UK. They all want to know about the great and wonderful Ember!" Sarah said, her voice low. I knew she must be on a break.

"What? People over there have heard about me?" I felt a tingle start in my toes and work its way up. Then it kind of simmered down when I thought about Graham. I wondered if he'd ever made it home then decided I didn't care. He wasn't a threat to me anymore, not with Kevin in my life.

"I guess so. They've asked all kinds of questions about you, but I keep telling them they'll have to wait until they see you to find out." Sarah was in her late twenties, with dark hair and a beautiful face that went with an even better body, but she didn't suffer fools lightly.

"I guess they're driving you up the wall then, huh?" I tapped a fingernail on the table as I waited for her to answer. The nail was manicured with a gel polish job that would have YouTubers screaming in envy; something else I'd never had before.

"They are, but I know it's good for business. I guess I better get back, I just wanted to tell you there are some foreigners here because of you." I heard her chuckle and laughed as we said goodbye.

Life really wasn't so bad.

I went down at the expected time, after a short nap and a refreshing shower, and did what I do best. I sang my heart out, and tonight, some of the loneliness I felt came through more than it often did. Being happy could make it hard to sing some of the sadder songs in my repertoire.

Kevin had given me that happiness. I didn't mind though, I'd just settled into the bar stool, closed my eyes until I heard the right note in my voice, and sang away. I had some happy songs, of course, but more than a few were sad, or at least bittersweet. I'd added a few to the set over the last few weeks, and the crowds seemed to love them.

Of course, they seemed to love anything I played. I swiped my hair out of my face and thanked the crowd for coming. They were all quiet, and I broke that silence with a slight joke at myself as I introduced the next song. It was the one I'd written for Kevin, and the crowd waited. I saw a few cell phones in the air and knew I was being recorded. It was something that had taken awhile to get used to.

I closed my eyes on the high notes and opened them on the lower ones. I saw a sea of faces, but none stood out to me. There was a group of women at the bar that had started to make a nuisance of themselves, but I ignored them. Probably an office getaway group or women on a bachelorette getaway weekend.

A hen do, that's what they called it in Britain, the thought entered my head as I sang on. An odd name for it, but whatever, I decided while the fiddler gave a little solo. I wondered if Kevin was out there. Then it was time for me to sing again, and I forgot about it, except for when the occasional scream came from that side of the bar.

Way too much fun, they'd regret it in the morning.

My set ended, and I went back to the dressing room to

wash my face down and rest for a minute. Sarah had already brought in a nice glass of lemonade and had left me a bottle of ice cold water. I needed it to soothe my throat after a night of singing. I broke the seal on the bottle of water and started to guzzle it as a knock came at the door.

"Heyyyy!" A strange woman with blonde hair and bright blue eyes walked in, even though I hadn't admitted her. "Girl, you are good."

I stood up, a little bemused that she'd made it backstage. "You're with those women at the bar."

I'd heard the English accent, she was one of the women in the group Sarah had told me about then.

"Yeah. We came all the way over here to see what Kevin's working on these days. Apparently, that's you." The woman had an oddly excited look in her eyes that set my nerves on edge, and I backed toward the door, my fists ready.

There was something hysterical in that gaze, and I didn't like it a bit. "Sorry, do you know Kevin?"

I heard my brain scream at me that I shouldn't provoke the woman, but maybe she wasn't as crazy as her eyes said she was.

"Oh yes, I know Kevin well. Very well. Threesome in bed with him well." She walked closer to me, and her voice went lower as she nodded. "Oh mate, did I know him well. I gave him everything he asked for, and he promised he'd get me a record contract. Guess what I got?"

"Chlamydia?" I don't know why it came out, but it did.

"What?" she asked, stumped for a moment.

"Chlamydia?" I said it more slowly. "I would have to

guess the result of such behavior was an STD, but I don't know. I've never done anything like that."

I was blocking out her words until she held up a picture of a baby, maybe two-years-old and smiling. "This is what I got. Did he tell you about that? Hmm?"

Suddenly those nights away jolted into my brain, and her words sank in. "He promised you he'd get you into music?"

My fingers were tight in my palms, but now they weren't fists to protect me; it was me trying not to scream as anger flushed through me.

"Yes, he did, love. Promised me the moon for a three-some, and I gave it to him. Stupidest thing I did."

"Why are you here then?" I asked, a knot in my throat as I stared her down. She was the model type, prettier than me, though the cake of makeup on her face was a little disgusting. I bet she couldn't put her face on a pillow without all of that rubbing off.

"Because. I wanted to see who he was about to do it to next. To warn you off. He won't admit this is his child; typical man, isn't he?" She didn't have to say anything else.

I couldn't abide men who avoided their responsibilities. Or women. "So where's your baby if you're over here wasting money on this endeavor?"

"He's with his nan, alright? My girlfriends and I decided to have a holiday, and I talked them in to coming here. I've heard about you, seen your videos. You aren't bad. But you don't deserve this."

I didn't want to believe her. I wanted to call her a liar, but she seemed so calm now, not crazy at all. I breathed in through my nose and back out. "Well, it's a good thing I'm in a better position then. No baby here. Thanks for the advice. Can you, uh, leave me alone now?"

"Sure, love. Thanks for listening. I thought you'd throw me out."

I probably should have, I'd thought, but smiled as I closed the door. What to do? I stared at myself in the mirror over my dressing table and tried to blink away the tears in my eyes. He had a kid he didn't take care of? That didn't seem like the man I knew, at all.

Maybe the baby wasn't his? He'd had a threesome with her though? That was just... a shiver passed through me. Kevin could be wild, but he'd never suggested anything like that with me. Did I not come off as the type, so he hadn't bothered?

I stared in the mirror and called myself a dozen kinds of a fool. I'd let another man into my heart, and look where it had got me. Did he even really plan a record?

I let my head sink into my arms, crossed on the dressing table, and sobbed as thoughts swirled in my head. Surely it wasn't all a lie? Please? Somebody, tell me the past three months weren't all a lie…

13

KEVIN

Kevin

I sank back into the seat of the jet and tried to relax. Lately, it seemed the only time I had to rest was when I was high in the air, on a jet, where my electronics had to be turned off for the duration of the flight. Well, they didn't have to be, but I pretended they did. It gave me an hour or two of quiet.

"Sir, would you like a drink?" I opened my eyes to see a flight attendant stood at the end of the row of seats.

"Just a ginger ale, please." I had another meeting as soon as I landed. I needed my head clear, even if it was after nine pm already.

I'd spent the last week going back and forth from London to Charlotte, then up to our branch in New York, down to Myrtle Beach and over to New Orleans to have a look at the bars in each one. I had a surprise for Ember when I got back to Nashville. Part of her new contract included exclusive tours of our bars throughout the world. I'd be going to Paris tomorrow, to check on our venue there to ensure it was up to par for my little songstress.

I'd taken full responsibility for Ember and the contract we had with her from day one, and now I took on this burden too. I could have passed it on to someone else, Mason and Trent had seen videos of Ember's talent and had agreed I'd been right about her, but I didn't trust anyone to make the right choices. I wanted everything to be perfect for her. That meant I had to do a lot of legwork.

Right about now Paula and Mark were going over the contract with Ember, and in a few days, I'd be back home with her. For a lot longer this time. I'd taken this on as my sole responsibility now; there wouldn't be anymore flying back and forth for the hotel. I'd made that deal with my brothers.

I sighed, happy with the world and all that had come to me with this woman. I was calm now, and maybe even a little more approachable than I normally was. She'd made me see that there was more to life than just getting through it so that I could die and get it all over with. That's how I'd been living, I realized now. As if I wanted to get out of life as quickly as I could.

Yeah, I'd found a lot of enjoyment in my life, but I hadn't had a goal or a dream. I'd just bounced around from task to task, and I wasn't doing any of that anymore. I knew what I wanted from life now, and that was Ember. For now, I knew she wanted to tour, to make music, and to experience life. She'd hidden from the world for so long, but now she didn't have to anymore. I was there to keep her safe.

I took a sip of the ginger ale and relaxed again. She'd even made me think about kids. I hadn't wanted kids before now, and had done my best to make sure I didn't have any, but with her? I found I wanted a little miniature version of that face of hers, or mine, to love and hold on to. So many of my male friends had changed when they had children that I'd wondered what fatherhood brought to them.

Was there something missing that I didn't know about? Was there some new emotion there that gave them that peace? Men who would normally get in fights and had done a lot of carousing suddenly turned into placid characters with a never-you-mind attitude. What had caused that?

I kind of liked the idea of Ember big with my baby too. I hadn't really thought about pregnant women before, not as sex partners, but the thought made me instantly hard, and I shifted in my seat to make sure my tray table hid me. Damn, where had that come from? I knew what I'd be doing in my hotel later tonight, if I didn't fall asleep first.

I chuckled to myself and took another swig of the ginger ale. Normally, that wasn't something that I would do, but without Ember, I'd become a pro at it. I'd wake up in the morning, hard as a rock and unable to do anything until I took care of it. At night, sometimes thoughts of her would keep me awake, and I'd have to do it again, as I remembered the sweet suction of her walls as I drove into her, or the way she sighed my name when she came apart.

Fuck, that wasn't helping the situation. The flight attendant came back and asked if I needed anything else. I was certain that might have been the first time I'd blushed since I was a schoolboy. I politely refused anything else, and tried to turn away from the older woman with dark red hair. She gave me a wink and sauntered off.

It was something I was used to. Women found me attractive and always had. Of course, I'd always found them attractive too, but I had Ember. I didn't need anyone else; in fact, I didn't want anyone else. Only her.

The flight soon ended, and I made my way to the next hotel. I had to wonder why my father had to build an empire that was spread out so far. He'd worked hard to build the business, but what had driven him to own so many hotels? Money was one thing, but this was a lot of work for one man to handle. He'd done it for a long time though, without our help, and I couldn't really be angry at him now.

We'd figured out it was all a ruse by now, his plan to get us under one roof to work together. He had never been sick. At first, I'd been more than a little angry with him, such a huge lie to tell, but he'd had his reasons. And for Mason and Trent, the ruse had brought them love, so could he really be blamed?

I still couldn't believe Mason was about to settle down with one woman, he just wasn't the kind, but he seemed to really love the woman who had stolen his heart. I was glad for him. Trent had kind of mellowed out too, since he'd finally admitted something we'd all known all along. He'd grown up with the woman he would one day fall in love with. Jessi was his perfect mate.

And I had mine. The jet finally landed, and I went to the bar just to get my land-legs back for a minute. I had a lot to get through today, so I ordered a cup of coffee and went over what I needed to get done again. I went and found the company car that would have been left for me and made my way to the hotel. It was in shambles, and my jaw dropped from the minute I stepped into the shabby car left for me until I drove up to the hotel. We hadn't been to this one for a while, and well, maybe the shape it was in was our own fault.

The exterior needed to be pressure washed, I could see one window was boarded up, and when I stepped in? I nearly lost my cool then, but managed to not fire everyone on the spot. The carpets were disgusting, the walls were grimy, and I could see staff members just leaning up against walls, chatting, as if one of the big guys hadn't just walked in. Maybe they didn't know who owned the place, but they were about to.

"I'm here to see the hotel manager," I told the young redhead at the counter, once she'd finally finished her phone conversation with her boyfriend. The name tag said her name was Jill.

"Oh, right, you're the big boss, aren't you?" She gave me a brief, but surly smile as she snapped her gum. "Let me just find out where Peter is."

By the time she picked up the phone again the bored

tone was back in her voice. Young Jill was definitely out of a job.

I managed to grit my jaw through the meeting and had made it back to my hotel without firing anyone before I actually felt my blood pressure start to calm down. I was angry at how poorly the bar was being managed and made notes to fire the old managers and hire new while the place was redecorated. *How could managers let our facilities run down like that?* I was even angrier when I saw stains on the duvet that should be pure white with a dark chocolate brown line toward the top. This would not do. I'd have to call Mason and Trent about this tomorrow.

For now, I ordered some room service, kicked off my shoes, and turned on the television to watch the late news. Images and words flashed, and I stared at the screen, but I didn't really notice any of it. Not really. My thoughts were on Ember. Room service came but my food was cold and tasted of sawdust, so I decided to get a flight back tonight. I couldn't stand anymore of the place.

I had my assistant find a flight for me and made ready to board another flight. Mason had the company jet, so I couldn't use that today. I was exhausted, grouchy, and wanted only to climb into bed with Ember. It would be late when I got in, but I didn't care. I just wanted to hold her. I hadn't seen her in almost two weeks now. It had been excruciating, but I'd managed to not spoil the surprise about the international tour I had planned for her.

That part wasn't in the contract, but it would be when I had it amended. By the time the plane had landed it was after one am, so I made my way to the hotel and quietly let myself into her room. I had a key of my own, so I didn't have to wake her when I came in late. From the moment I opened the door I knew she wasn't there.

The lights were on, but things were missing. The blanket she'd hid under when she watched movies on the couch was gone. The picture she'd hung up on the wall was missing too.

"Ember?" I called out, but I could tell she wasn't there. I wanted to pretend I'd come into the wrong room, but I saw a note on the table in the kitchen. It had my name on it.

I stared at it for a few minutes as I sank into a chair. I didn't want to open it. I wanted to pound my fist into the table, but I didn't want to gain a destructive reputation like Mason had. I slid cold, numb fingers across the table and picked up the envelope finally, and opened it.

"I'm done. Don't look for me. Leave me alone. Thanks. Ember."

That was all it took to make my world crumble around me. A few lines, not even a paragraph really. Just a few lines, and all of my plans for the future, all of the hopes I'd started to build, were gone. I stared at the paper, dry-eyed and hollow inside.

I wasn't sure what I was supposed to feel. I felt numb. Betrayed. Confused. So I did the only thing I could do at that point. I slid off my shoes, slid into the bed that still smelled of her, and wrapped my arms around her pillow. I blocked it all out and went to sleep rather than face the music. Or lack of it. There was a definite lack of music now. I might never listen to it again.

A restless night left me achy and grouchy the next day. I

didn't know what to do with myself. All of my work centered around Ember, all of my plans, all of the tasks I had to do, had hinged on her. And she'd fucked off.

It was really hitting me this morning. The rest of my team hadn't figured it out yet, but they would soon enough so I called a meeting. I wanted to run away, to head up into the mountains and hike this ache away, or climb rocks until the pain in my body and fingers surmounted the pain in my heart, but I had an obligation to my family to help run this business.

"Paula, I need you to find another act to replace Ember. It seems she won't be signing a new contract with us for now. Mark, you need to help her out. Sarah, can you take down all of the notifications about Ember's times on our social media platforms? And the posters here in the hotel, take those down too." I could see a row of shocked faces in front of me, a row of faces with questions, but they could tell from my tone I had no answers.

For the first time in my life, my heart was broken and nobody could fix it. I thought about calling my mom or Emily, but I'd always done my own thing. I was never really close to any of my family, and I didn't want to start opening myself up now. It might hurt too much.

Words beat inside of my head, to the pace of my heart-beat, over and over again, without end. She was gone.

I had no idea why or where she'd gone, but she had. Her note made it clear that she was done with me.

"Are you alright, Kevin?" Sarah asked, and I smiled at the young woman. Leave it to the toughest looking one to notice when someone else was in pain.

"Just tired, Sarah, but thanks. Any questions?" I knew there wouldn't be but gave them a chance, just in case. When they all shook their heads I dismissed them.

What purpose did I have now? I decided I needed a drink. A drink where nobody could judge me or report to my father about it. I picked up the phone and made one very long distance call to an old friend in England. It only rang once before he answered.

"Kevin? Hey, what's up, mate?" I heard Henry's voice as clear as if he was right beside of me, but he wasn't.

"Ah, you know how it is, Hen, some days are your days, some days you need to borrow an old friend's cabin in the woods to lick your wounds." I knew I could be open with Henry. We'd been best mates in school, and the bastard son of a king was a generous kind of guy. He also had a cabin near some rocks I loved to climb, and wouldn't refuse my request.

"You know where the keys are, Kevin. That bad is it?" I heard sympathy in his voice and knew I'd made the right choice.

"It's pretty bad, yeah. Who knew love could you fuck you up like this?" It wasn't something I'd planned to admit, but I had so I let it go.

"Things are never black and white are they?" Henry, a wise guy for a playboy bastard prince, said with a chuckle of commiseration. "Use the place as long as you need it. Let me know when you're done, and I'll send the cleaners in."

"Thanks, Henry, I really appreciate it. You coming over this way soon?" It had been a few months since I'd last seen him and told him all about the most incredible woman I'd only just met.

"I don't know. I have a few things on my plate, but I might. Take care, my friend. I have to go, but you enjoy those rocks. Later." Henry hung up then, and I took a deep breath. I closed down my laptop, my phone, and packed a bag for my time at the mountain hideaway.

Henry's dad owned properties around the world, this cabin in the mountains was one he'd given to Henry as a token of love. Henry's father might not have married his mother, but he cared for his son and his son's mother very much. If only Ember had loved me that way.

14

KEVIN

Kevin

Bleary sunlight broke through a window as I cracked an eyelid open a week later. Something had woken me up.

"Kevin!" I heard the sound of my name and a fist against a door.

"What the fuck?" I said, but said it quietly. My head was thumping.

I stood up and kicked away the bottles of beer and knocked over a half-empty bottle of whiskey that some idiot had left teetering on a side table as I made my way to the door. The fact that I'd been alone all week meant that idiot was me. I was going to have to hire cleaners when I left.

The fist against the door wouldn't let up, and I almost got a fist in the face when I pulled the wooden door open. "Emily? What are you doing here?"

My cool, calm, and collected sister swept in, her blonde hair neatly in place, and her eyes a glare I couldn't look away from.

"Where have you been? And where's Ember?" She looked me over, a grown man still in his boxer shorts, hair in fifty directions with a beard on his chin and a glaze in his eyes.

"I've been here. And fuck if I know where Ember is." I glared back at her, defensive, angry, and not ready for this confrontation yet. I'd known it was coming, every night I'd drunk myself to sleep. I'd known it was coming, I'd just hoped it would take a little bit longer than this to get here.

"You can't just leave without telling us you know?" Her hand was on her hip, a sure sign she was in a bossy mood. Emily was always in a bossy mood when it came to her brothers, though. She'd bossed all of us, even Trent, from the day she was born, in one way or another.

"Why the hell not? I'm not Dad's slave you know? Sometimes people need time off," I grumbled, but when she just kept up that glare, I waved my hand and walked away. I needed coffee for this.

"You have to tell us because we're your family, Kevin. You had meetings you didn't show up for, and Ember's disappeared. We were all kind of worried about you…" Her words trailed off, and I narrowed my eyes at her.

"Are you trying to imply you thought she killed me? Are

you insane?" I poured coffee into the basket and filled the back up with water. "She wouldn't hurt me…"

But she had hurt me. That was why I was out here in this cabin, with no idea where my clothes or shoes were. And that horrible taste in my mouth, fuck, how much had I downed last night?

"I finally got Henry on the phone, and he told me where you were. He said something was wrong, but he thought you'd be alright. You stopped answering your phone, so I wanted to be sure."

"Well," I paused to roll a beer bottle out of my way, "as you can see, I'm fine. Now piss off."

I probably shouldn't have been so harsh with my sister. She only came out here because she cared, but part of me wanted to tell her to piss off again. The only reason she'd come out was because she wanted to boss me around. I could see it on her face. Then, the glare softened, and she looked me over.

"Why don't you come home? I don't know what's happened, but obviously you're at a low. Come back and let us help you." She had changed tactics.

"I'll be back when I'm ready. Until then, just leave me be." I knew she was right, I needed to get out of my funk, but I couldn't face it at the moment.

I couldn't face a world without Ember in it. That's why I was out in the woods, away from everything and everyone I knew. I didn't have to hear her name out here, although I thought it a million times a day. I didn't have to see pictures of her online, even if I couldn't forget her face.

Nobody asked me about her out here, but the sad part was, I couldn't stop thinking about her anyway.

Maybe Emily was right.

"Fine. I'll drive back this evening." I headed to the shower and was surprised when I came out to find Emily was still there, typing on her phone. "What's up?"

"I thought you might want someone to talk to." Her eyes, so similar to mine but softer, definitely feminine, looked up at me with patience.

"About what?" I rubbed the towel through my hair and tried not to look at her.

"About Ember. What happened?"

"She's gone. I don't know where. Basically, she said, thanks for the memories, and fucked off. I haven't seen her or heard from her since I came back from my trip."

"She said that?" Emily was on the edge of her seat now.

"I'm just as confused as you are. I went to her room, and she'd left me a note on the table. No explanation, just a see ya." I sat down on the recliner beside the couch and looked down at my hands. "I don't know if she was just a gold digger, or if somebody spooked her, but something happened."

"But you're the one who offered everything to her, Kev. You can't call her a gold digger when you barely even gave her a choice." Emily looked a bit miffed over that, and her eyebrow lifted.

Oh no, dodgy ground. "Well, yes, you're right. I did just kind of barrel through…"

"And did you bother to actually ask her what she

wanted before you just did it most of the time? You didn't, did you? You just plan things and then want to surprise people. She probably had no clue what was going on in her life half the time." Emily shook her head and looked at me with disbelief.

I couldn't say she was wrong, but I didn't think I'd been wrong either. "Emily, she never had the opportunities we had. She didn't grow up with privilege, how would she know what to do? I just took away the embarrassment of not knowing from her."

"No, you took her choice away, Kevin. Dang, no wonder she left! Did you just pity her?"

"No! She taught me that what I'd been given was special; it was something I shouldn't waste. I could have been her, playing for peanuts in a park, if I hadn't been born into this family. But I was, and she taught me what it was like to be delighted with life again." I sighed and sat back. "God, you should have seen her when I took her shopping. It was like a kid in a candy store."

"But did you let her pick out what she wanted?" Emily with that raised eyebrow again.

"I pointed out some outfits for her performances, but otherwise, she chose what she wanted, yes."

"That was a start then. So there was no fight or anything? She just left?"

"She wasn't there when I came home. I hadn't talked to her in about two weeks." I felt those eyes burn into me again, but I didn't look up. "So no, there was no fight."

"Where could she be?"

"Our contract was up, maybe she took up someone else

on their offer?" That snide little brat in me came to life and said she'd climbed over me to get a better deal, but the grown man in me told that brat to shut the fuck up. She wasn't that kind.

"But our deal was supposed to be one of the best ever offered to a new talent like hers..." Emily started, but I looked away again, shame on my face.

"I hadn't told her yet. I, uh, wanted to surprise her when I got home."

"Jesus, Kev! You let her contract run out without talking to her about it? What kind of dick are you?" She was on her feet now, and I couldn't blame her, not one bit. My behavior did seem a bit stupid now.

"I'm sorry, Emily. I, like you said, I like the surprise part." Maybe it had cost me more than I'd wanted to give, just to surprise her. She'd surprised me instead.

"How serious are you about her?" Emily asked suddenly.

"I want to marry her. I even bought her ring while I was in England." I wagged a finger toward a velvet box on the coffee table in front of us. "I guess I won't need it now."

"You might not. Let me make some calls, see if we can figure out where she is, at least. We owe her that much."

"We owe her a lot more than that. She showed me the world could be a much better place, Emily. A place that's beautiful. I just... I want her back."

Emily looked at me with sad eyes before she stood up and offered a hug. I took the embrace and gave it back. "Hold tight, brother. I'll see what I can do."

The drive to Nashville jarred me back into reality. I

passed small towns that were barely hanging on, yet families still kept their lawns cleared and managed. I'd never known a hard day in my life, not like some of these families had known. I'd never had to decide between medicine and food, dying so that I could eat, or going to the doctor to find out why I was ill. I'd never had to put off owning something until I could save for it. I'd never lived without because I could never dream of affording it. Ember had shown me that world, and even with the money that she'd made from her job with us, she was still frugal, as if it all might escape from her one day without notice.

Ember had shown me that people struggled to feed themselves. Sometimes because of bad decisions that left them with no options, and sometimes because a good decision goes drastically wrong. I'd never really thought people chose to be homeless, but she'd been in a situation beyond anything I'd heard of before. What would have happened to her if I hadn't come along? Would she have been deported?

I didn't know, but these were things people should know, maybe. So often the less fortunate were shown magazines and programs about the life of the filthy rich, and I'd often wondered why? Was it to encourage them to work harder, or was it that people were so obtuse they didn't realize not all moms in a checkout line couldn't afford the magazine much less the palaces showcased within?

Sure, it was nice to daydream sometimes, but did we constantly have to charge premium prices for crap and shove it in people's faces? I'd been in a magazine a time or two because of some charity event I'd been to or just out with a friend for the night. I'd never thought anything of it, other than it was an annoyance. And what really hit me was the fact that I'd never asked what charity I'd supported with my money. It was just something my crowd did, and we never asked how the money was spent or where it went to. For all I know, it could line some executive's pocket.

She'd made me think about all of these things, and I'd stupidly, selfishly thrown it all away. I had to assume. Ember loved me, I could see it in her face when she looked at me, though she'd never said it. She didn't have to, I could read it in her eyes. She wouldn't have thrown that away for any amount of money or fame.

She'd had a hard life. She still didn't talk to her mom because the woman had done such a poor job of being a mother. What kind of life must that have been? I couldn't imagine hating my mother, and I was sure Ember didn't hate hers, but she certainly didn't feel she owed the woman anything. I couldn't imagine feeling that toward my mother.

My mom was a bit of a socialite, but she'd never been terrible. Ember's mother had left her to fend for herself in more ways than one from the moment she was born. Her ex-boyfriend had wanted to use her but couldn't figure out how to. When that had failed, he'd tried to force her to be a drug mule. She'd only known love from one person, her grandmother, and that poor woman had left her early. She wouldn't have left me for money.

I was an idiot for thinking otherwise, but I knew it now. I had to find her and find out why she left. I punched a button on the car's cellular system and told it to dial Emily. "Have you found anything yet?"

"No, we're still looking. I'll let you know if I hear anything." Emily sounded distracted, so I didn't keep her.

"Alright. Thanks, Emily. Talk to you later."

I made it back to the hotel in Nashville, and part of me hoped Ember would have come home by now, but the room was still empty. I went down to the bar and found Sarah there. "Hi, Sarah. Ginger ale, please."

"Coming up. You heard from Ember?" She didn't look at me directly, so I knew she had tried to be polite about it. The two had become friends, and if anyone would have known where Ember was, Sarah would have. The fact that she hadn't made me worry.

"No, what happened? She was gone when I came back from England." I took a sip of the drink she'd slid over the bar and waited.

"I don't know. Things looked normal that last night. She sang her heart out, as always, and then this group of women came in from England. Started asking me about her, kind of snide you know? The next thing I know, one of them had slipped in the back to find Ember backstage. By the time I figured it out and went to go pull her out, she was leaving Ember's dressing room. That was the last time I saw Ember."

Cold waves of rage washed over me. "An English woman? Did she look like this?"

I scrolled through my phone until I found the picture I

wanted. A picture from a detective I'd hired two years ago. When the woman started to stalk me.

"Yeah, her hair was more blonde than this, but that's her."

Damnit. The crazy stalker was back.

15

EMBER

Ember

I want to go home. The thought hit me as I stared out the window of the tiny apartment I'd rented in New York City, cold rain streaks on the steamy glass. I was so… lonely.

It'd only been a little over a week since I left Nashville, so I knew I had to give the place a chance, but it was so noisy and frightening. Of course, I'd made my way in London, but that had been different. I'd expected everything to seem foreign; they drove on the wrong side of the road didn't they? Here? It was the same country, but everything was just so very different.

There were cabs everywhere, people and machines constantly made noise, and there always seemed to be a frantic pace to life. Get there, get here, quickly, quickly, before time runs out. Was that a zest for life, or a fear that life would pass them by before they knew it? I couldn't decide and left my seat in the window to head deeper into the loft.

I'd used the money I had saved in my account to rent this place and was about to sign a contract with an agent. I didn't want to, but it was the best offer I'd been made so I had decided to take it. I'd make a record, go on tour, and the world would be at my feet, or so I'd been told. I had a feeling that promise had been made to more than one artist.

I had to give this place time, I reminded myself. No, I hadn't made any friends yet, but I would. In time. When the pain over Kevin didn't cut me anymore.

He'd turned out to be no better than Graham. How could he leave a child like that, his own child, without a father? I bet he didn't even send the mother child support. Sure, he could spend thousands on me, and promise me the moon, but if I got pregnant would his tune change? Would I suddenly become someone he didn't know?

I'd seen all those talk shows where men denied their babies, claimed they never even had sex with the mother. I knew how often they turned out to be liars. Every now and then a woman was proven to be a fraud, but not very often. More often than not, the man tried to get away with it. I didn't know why, DNA testing had been around for decades; didn't they know the test could prove the truth?

It all made me very sad, so I sprawled out on the mattress I'd flopped down on the floor as a bed. I crawled under my duvet, pulled it over my head, and tried to block out the world. It didn't work.

I wanted to talk to Sarah, to ask her advice, but I had a feeling I knew what she'd say. I didn't even give him a chance. She hadn't been in my shoes though. She hadn't had the life I'd had. She didn't know what it was like, but then, I told myself I'd jumped to conclusions. I didn't know everything in Sarah's past, or how she'd grown up. I didn't know her experience with lovers.

Maybe she'd had as many bad experiences as I'd had. I was surprised when my phone started to vibrate on my nightstand. It was Sarah. She'd tried to call me every day since I'd left the bar in Nashville. I'd ignored the calls and texts from her and others since that day. I'd wanted to break all ties, but I felt a tug toward Sarah.

She'd been so nice to me, so sweet. I couldn't leave her like that.

"Hey," I answered, my voice breathless. "How are you?"

"I'm alright. You know me. How are you?" She sounded concerned, but she didn't push me.

"I'm… okay. Just a little far from home." I had been since I'd left Alabama, truth be told. That was why I was so hurt over all of this.

I'd started to plan a future, with a home, a real home, and that woman had made me see that Kevin hadn't had those kinds of plans. He'd never talked about the future anyway, so what kind of plans could he have had, really? It was best I popped that little bubble of a dream now and get it over with.

"Where are you?" Sarah asked, and I sighed, not sure what to tell her.

"I'm in New York. But please, don't tell anybody." It wasn't like Kevin had called me or texted me anyway. For all I knew he hadn't come back from the last trip he was on. He might not even know I was gone yet. The hotel would though, and surely someone would have informed him.

"I won't. Listen, Kevin's back, and he's looking for you." She paused, and I could tell she was trying to decide what to say next. "Look, I don't know what happened, and you don't have to tell me, but if it had anything to do with those British women who were here, I don't think you can trust anything they might have said."

"Oh." I went to roll over and promptly fell out of the bed, onto the floor. Another reason not to have a bed frame. I picked up the phone where I'd dropped it and answered again. "I just thought it was time to try something new."

"Alright." I heard her say to my lie. "Well, in that case, Kevin's looking for you, but I won't tell him where you are. I wouldn't do that to you. Are you okay up there?"

"I am, just lonely and bored. I guess when I start work on the album I won't be bored anymore, but right now, while I wait, it's killing me." I stood up and went into the kitchen. I still had at least a glass of wine left in that box I'd brought from Tennessee with me, and it was calling my name.

Kevin was looking for me? Why? I'd told him not to. Why couldn't men actually listen when a woman spoke?

I set the phone down as Sarah relayed Kevin's sudden reappearance, tilted the plastic dispenser on the box of wine, and filled my glass. The sweet smell of muscadine grapes filled the air, and I felt calm pour through me quickly.

Nothing could be bad as long as I had muscadine wine.

I took a sip and went into the living room area. Just a couch, two chairs, and a table in the broader expanse of the giant room I called an apartment. At least the bathroom and bedroom were separate. Sort of. The bedroom was formed from dressing screens, and not really a room at all. The bathroom did have a door though. The rest was all open.

"Are you going to stay up there then?" She'd paused, and I realized I hadn't said anything at all.

"I don't plan on coming back, no. I guess I'm like a gypsy, aren't I? No roots and nowhere to call home. My home is the world." I'd tried to make Kentucky home, but that hadn't been very nice. London had only been a temporary home. I'd tried to set up a home in Tennessee. I'd even started to look at houses I could rent in Nashville, but nothing serious.

This apartment was the first home I'd ever provided for myself, and I had to make the best of it. Somehow.

"Well, I don't want to lose touch with you, so don't forget me, okay?" Sarah sounded as if she had tears in her voice, and I was shocked. "I really hate that you aren't here. You brought so much sunshine into the world, you know?"

"Well, it's not like I'm dead, silly. You can come visit me. Or we can meet halfway at some point." I took another sip of wine and smiled. "Maybe you can go on tour with me, be my resident bartender."

"Oh, you only like that horrible wine of yours. I'd never make a good bartender for you." She laughed, and I felt relieved. Tears and crisis averted!

"You might, you never know." I took one more sip and put the glass down. "Now, tell me what's happening with everybody. What's the gossip?"

We settled into a long chat about the new girl that had taken my place and how she only had a one month contract; she'd been next on the list. Something about that made me cringe, I didn't like knowing someone else was on my stage.

At least she wasn't singing my songs.

"I tell you, Mark's gone stupid over her, but I think it had more to do with what's in her shirt than what she sings. She's not as good as you, and her lyrics are kind of, well, boring."

"Well, thank you for that ego boost. I needed it." I laughed and wiped a tear from my eye. Sarah could be very cutting when it came to other people.

"No problem. Hey, listen, if you ever want to come back, you know you have a place at my house, right? I've always got room." Sarah had been left the house she'd grown up in when her parents died in a car accident. She didn't have to pay rent, and the house had five bedrooms. More than enough for guests.

"I appreciate that. Maybe one day." When I didn't want to avoid Kevin anymore, when the hurt was gone.

"Thanks. I'm going to get back to work now. You take care of yourself, Ember. I'll call you again soon."

I thanked her for thinking of me and turned the phone off. At least someone wanted me to come back. I stuck my thumbnail between my teeth and chewed at a hangnail. Why was Kevin on the hunt for me? Did he want me to pay him back since I'd left him before he was finished playing with me?

No, he'd never said anything that would make me think he wanted repayment. In fact, he'd been explicit with the fact that he didn't want to be repaid. I'd left with a clear conscience on that front, at least. Maybe I should have given him a chance to explain himself, but I hadn't wanted to.

So many times Graham had sweet talked me into ignoring behaviors and actions that should have sent me running. I'd take a deep breath, shut my eyes, and force the problem to the back of my mind. I didn't ever want to do that again and refused to do it with Kevin.

Which is why I was mad at myself for rolling over when Kevin would disappear on his business trips. Okay, I always knew where he told me he was, but how did I know any of that was true? He'd cut off all communication in the times when he was gone.

I didn't think he had other women, but I thought he had a life outside of our relationship. One that meant he couldn't take us seriously, or he'd have tried a little bit harder to call me, to not leave me so lonely.

I hadn't said it to Sarah, but all I wanted to do was run back to Nashville. I'd come to love the city, the place where

I lived and worked, and Kevin. I mainly wanted to run back to him, but I was trying to hold my resolve. I went to the kitchen for another glass of wine to fortify myself with.

I missed him so much. I missed the way I felt in his arms, the way he made me laugh uncontrollably, and the things he did when we were in bed. I missed that part a lot. My body craved his touch, and right now, I felt as if I was going through withdrawals after being away from him for so long.

Could you be addicted to a person? In a non-codependent sort of way? I didn't think you could, but my body said otherwise. More than once since I'd moved in I'd found myself staring at the key ring that hung just by the door on a rack. I'd never learned to drive, but I had keys to my door, the one downstairs, and to the mailbox below.

I could just leave those in the owner's mailbox and walk away. I didn't care about deposits, not really. I could always make more money, but could I live with myself if I gave in? Would he even want me back after I'd left him like that? I doubted it, I hadn't even let him explain the situation.

"But that's giving him credit where it might not be deserved," I said out loud to myself.

Kevin had been different from Graham, in many respects. I can't say they were a matching set, not at all. They did share similar qualities though. Graham hadn't let me make decisions because he thought I was stupid. Kevin hadn't because he liked to surprise people. Graham had never hid a child from me, but I knew he'd be the kind to ignore paternity suits and a child if he had one. We'd made very sure I couldn't get pregnant, something I'd hated at the time, but now I was glad I hadn't tied myself to him in that way.

To either of them.

I wanted to cry again because now I wondered if I'd ever find a man to have kids with. I wanted babies, little sprouts of love to cuddle and raise until they turned into teenagers who hated you. I wanted that experience, though. I guessed I'd just have to wait a little longer.

I know there's a man out there for me, one who will check all the right boxes. I thought that man had been Kevin, but now I knew differently. There'd never be a future with a man like that. Not for me, anyway.

With a huge sigh, I found the remote, sipped at the glass in my other hand, and tried to find a movie to watch to pass the time.

I had to move on with my life. That had been easy to do when it came to Graham, but it was proving a lot harder with Kevin. I was sure many would have said I should have been glad for the experience, and in a way, I was, but in others, I wasn't. I really didn't need to be taught a lesson on how fragile my heart was, I'd known that my entire life after all.

It would have been nice if Kevin had been the one. I could have died happily with the life we could have made. But it wasn't meant to be. Somehow, I had to get used to that.

16

KEVIN

Kevin

"Isn't that the wrong direction to be heading in?" I heard Emily's voice through the car speakers and smiled.

"It probably is, but Mason's made a fool of himself more than once. He knows how to make up for being a dick."

"Well, I'm sure that language isn't necessary, but I know what you mean." *Since when was my sister a prude,* I thought, but let it go.

"Are you going to go to New York after you see Mason?" Emily prodded. She wanted me to get Ember back for two reasons. The club's audience did not like the new entertainer, and she wanted me happy.

"I might. I don't know yet. I'll see what Mason thinks. I'm almost there; let me go, Emily. You know this part always gets difficult." I was heading toward an area with a lot of traffic lights and heavy traffic, so I needed all of my attention on the road.

I navigated the traffic with ease after that and soon arrived at our hotel in Myrtle Beach. Mason was down here to be with his girlfriend and wanted me to report on what had happened. In person.

He hadn't sounded happy on the phone, but just as he'd said to Trent once before in his life, Mason was not the boss of me. He could question my decisions, but I was in charge of entertainment, not him.

I found him in an office to himself, no assistant in sight. "What's up, Mason?" I called out and he turned to me with a smile.

"Kevin. Thanks for coming."

It was odd to see my sporty brother in a suit and tie, but there he sat, blond hair clean and gray eyes clear. Far from the bleary-eyed drunk I'd seen on too many occasions. "Take a seat."

He made my eyebrow quirk with that, and then he laughed. "Sorry, still getting used to being in charge. Now, what's going on?"

Straight and to the point. Good.

"I guess I played by your rule book and fucked up."

"What do you mean?" Mason didn't skip a beat.

"I wanted my cake and to eat it too. I let the woman that everything depends on get away."

"So you fucked her and broke her heart, is that it?" Mason, always direct.

"I, no. I planned on asking her to marry me, actually." I

pulled the box out of my pocket, where I always kept it. "It's the crazy lady. She got in the way."

"I thought we took care of Veronica?" Mason asked, confused about a subject he thought we'd sorted well over a year ago.

"Seems not. DNA proved what I'd said all along, the baby wasn't mine; I'd never even met the woman. A psychiatric evaluation showed she was delusional, but I guess she was off her meds or something, I don't know. I do know the night she showed up at the bar in Nashville, Ember left."

"You have to get her back. And I hate to sound harsh, but not just for your sake. Her loss is hurting our bottom line. The hotel was booked solid until it was announced we'd changed singers."

"I know, I've seen the cancellation data. I'm not going to try to get her back for that, though. To be honest, fuck the empire. I just want Ember." I sank into the luxurious leather chair and stared off into space. "I have never felt like that about a woman before. I don't want to feel this way about another either. I only want to feel it for her. Ever."

"Then you have it bad, brother. Do what you have to, for your own sake. I shouldn't have put that kind of weight on you." His words made my head jerk around to observe him.

"That woman of yours had changed you," I said without derision.

"I know. It's a good thing. I'd have been dead before I learned my lesson, the way I was going. She's just..."

"Brought meaning to an empty life?" I provided. Yeah, that's exactly how I felt about Ember.

"Exactly. Now, go on, go get something done. I just hope you can get her back. She's about to sign with another company from what Emily said."

"You talked about this with Emily?" That was kind of rude.

"It's the family business, of course I did, brother. Now, seriously, Monday she's going to sign contracts we can't get her out of. Hurry."

"I might not be able to convince her that quickly."

"You're the man for her. You're a Thompson, any woman would be lucky to have you. And if she's that great, then you're lucky to have her. Now, get the fuck out of my office." Mason laughed, the kind of laugh I've never heard from him.

It actually sounded happy for a change, not his usual self-deprecating or sarcastic laugh. Laura had been good for him, I decided.

The way Ember had been good for me.

I got back on the phone the moment I was out of the office and called my PA to order plane tickets. I'd see her, tonight. If Emily had Ember's location, that is. NYC was a big place; it might be impossible to find her before Monday.

I only had a short time to find her though. I didn't care if we launched her career or not, but the deal she'd made with these new people might not make it possible to spend much time with her. Would they look after her health?

I realized I was already micromanaging and told myself

to stop as I headed for an airport nearby. I dropped the car off with the rental agency and headed for my flight. I had a little bit of a wait and took the call from Henry when it came through.

"Did you go to the cabin, mate?" I heard him ask in my ear. I had my headphones on to keep the conversation private, at least on his end.

"I did, yeah. Why?" I was confused, but I had called a cleaner in, so that shouldn't have been a problem.

"The cleaner says there was nothing for her to do. It was already spotless." Henry laughed, and I had to laugh with him.

"Yeah, I sent in my own cleaner. I was there for about a week, and made a little bit of a mess, so I thought a cleaner was the least I could do. Thanks, man. It wasn't the healthiest time for me, but it was what I needed at the moment."

"I hope you are going to try to get this woman back, Kevin. This life, it's getting old, isn't it? Sure, easy sex and no wife mean life is uncomplicated, but it's hollow isn't it? I'm starting to feel a little lonely."

"Aw, come on, we aren't that old." I laughed. Henry made it sound like life had passed us by.

"No, but I think it's time we both tried to settle down, don't you?" Henry had a point.

"I'm trying. If this works, I'll be the next in line for wedding bells."

"I'll hold you to that. Now, if you have anyone in mind for me, just let me know. I haven't found one yet."

"I'm sure there's someone out there for you." I heard my

flight called over the speaker. "My flight is boarding. I'll call you soon, Henry. Wish me luck."

It was Friday night, and the sun had already gone down by the time my plane took off. Emily hadn't returned my calls yet, and all I knew was I needed to go to New York City. She'd found out that much.

What would I do when I got there? I'd have to find a way to locate her. I couldn't just go around to apartments and ask for Ember, now could I? I decided to go to the hotel until I heard from Emily. It was all I could do really. Especially now that I was exhausted.

I had a lot of beer to get out of my system too, and a lot of sleepless nights to make up for. It wasn't a surprise when I got to my room that I fell asleep. What was a surprise was what I dreamed about.

I'd become used to sex dreams about Ember; she fulfilled all of my fantasies in real life so it wasn't a surprise I dreamed sexy dreams about her. What did surprise me was dreaming about a wedding day with her.

In the dream we were in a large cathedral, and she had started to make her way down the aisle. She was in a pale white dress with light purple flowers in her hand, some variety I couldn't identify, with a train that trailed out behind her for a long way. She was beautiful, heavenly, and I couldn't imagine when she'd ever looked more beautiful.

As always, she didn't have a lot of makeup on, and her skin was free of the substance that I actually hated. The concealer stuff that came off on everything. She never wore it, and it was one of the things I liked about her. She would enhance her eyes with eyeliner, eyeshadow, and sometimes mascara, especially on stage, but that was about all. It was all she wore now. With just enough lip gloss to make her lips soft and wet looking, she was the most gorgeous woman I'd ever seen.

The priest, which was odd because we weren't even Catholic, started to speak and the crowd went quiet. I couldn't hear a word the man said, however, because all I could focus on was the brown depths of Ember's eyes.

This beautiful young woman was about to become my wife, and I couldn't have been more proud. She'd chosen me, which was unbelievable. I didn't deserve her.

And then we were on our way down the aisle, two new gold bands on our fingers, and smiles wreathing our faces. Throughout the entire day, which wasn't long because it was a dream and time jumped around, all I could see was her face and eyes. Even when she leaned in to speak to me, all I could concentrate on was the way she smelled and the heat of her skin against mine.

We danced at one point, swayed together in perfect time. It was magic. What else could have been better?

Our wedding night came, a nice quiet cabin on a desolate island with pure white sand. Sand so white it looked like snow when the moon rose. Ember was on the beach in a long white cotton dress, her hair blown by the breeze. She started to walk away, into the sea, and I followed her.

I heard my voice, but didn't know if I'd spoke or not. She didn't stop, so maybe I only thought the sentence. "Where are you going, Ember?"

I felt the tug of sand and water at my feet, and I wanted her to stop, but she was too far ahead. I did the only thing I could do, and I followed her deeper into the water. Soon, it was over my head, and I kicked my legs and stroked my arms into the water, but I didn't see her now. I dove beneath the waves, but I couldn't find her.

I drove through the water, my eyes open despite the sting of salt, and tried to locate her. Above me, waves continued to crash, and the surge took me back toward the beach. I kicked back out into the depths and surged through waves until I was in calmer waters. I had to come up for air. My lungs were on fire, and I was about to pass out. I didn't want to stop my search, but I needed air. I broke the surface of the water and gasped in a lungful of air. I swiped at the water on my face and looked around. She wasn't on the surface, nothing broke the solid midnight blue of the ocean lit only by the full moon.

Then, I looked back toward the beach, and she was there. Naked as she waited for me. How had she got back there? When had her hair dried? I was confused, but happy to see her alive and on the beach. Safe, she was safe there.

I swam back to her, and she laughed as she ran into the house. I caught up to her and covered her face in kisses. My playful joy soon turned to passion, and I let my fingers trail down her side until I found that round part of her ass and snugged her into my hips. I knew she could feel how hard I was, how eager I was to be inside her.

Those sweet walls that I'd missed so much would suck me in, wrap me in liquid heat, and hold me inside of her with ease. Her fingers grasped at my shoulders as she twisted beneath me, and at last, I could hear her voice. She panted my name, over and over again, until I quickly found the center of her, hot and wet for me, and drove into her.

I thought I'd die the minute I sank into her. So exquisite, that sensation of being tightly wrapped in hot, velvety honey. Fuck, it was so good. I buried my head in her neck and we moved together, over and over as our bodies fought to find that heavenly place meant only for the two of us.

I rolled and then she was on top of me. I loved it when she was on top of me like that. Her hair always brushed at my thighs in the most enticing ways, and she would writhe on top of me in her own way. Her hips moved, and I found her clit with one hand and a nipple with the other.

I watched her explode on me, and I knew this was the most perfect thing we could ever do together. Sex was when we were absolute magic.

I woke up from the dream suddenly, my dick hard and my body on fire. I didn't have paper and pen, so I pulled up a notepad on my phone and began to write. I wrote songs when I was in a band, but stopped when the band dissolved and then my dad insisted I become more involved with the hotels. I hadn't had a reason to write another song since then, and even now, my attempts might have seemed sophomoric compared to the songs Ember could just magic up off the top of her head. But it was a song I wanted to sing on our wedding day. If only I could find her.

EMBER

Ember

Maybe I was crazy, but I'd put off signing the contract. I had this crawly feeling all over my skin every single time I considered putting my name on it. Tied to people I didn't know, with clauses I didn't understand wasn't a very smart thing to do, was it? I knew this was my gut telling me this wasn't a good deal.

Oh, it looked like it, the contract promised me the moon and stars, but something was just... off. I probably should've had a lawyer look it over, maybe that would've helped. I tapped my thumbnail against my bottom teeth and stared at the hard copy of the contract. I knew some of my problem was the fact that I wanted to go back to Nashville.

I loved the cozy atmosphere there, the growing legion

of fans I had, and the way my voice rang through the room just right. I loved my room back there, and that bed. God, I missed that bed. There was also the fact that I couldn't find muscadine wine up here. I could find reds and whites from all over the world, but not a single drop of muscadine. What was that about?

And Kevin was there. I'd felt as if I'd held my breath all weekend as I waited for him to show up. I hadn't seen him though, and I'd started to think I wouldn't. I'd been a little apprehensive when Sarah had said Kevin was on the prowl, but that had soon passed. Maybe I'd made a mistake, after all?

A big part of relationships was trust. There had to be trust, or so all of the blogs I'd read had said. You had to trust your partner, and they had to trust you. I hadn't done that though. Instead, I'd trusted some woman I didn't know from Adam, and had run off like the Runaway Bride. Spooked at the first sign of trouble.

We hadn't even had our first argument yet! And here I was, about to put my life in some stranger's hands to protect myself from what? A broken heart that I'd given to myself. Maybe I should have waited, asked him. I wouldn't be up here in this cold, noisy place that made me feel like a small cog in a galaxy-sized machine.

I pushed the contract away and went back to my window. I'd called the agent's office and told them I didn't feel well. Such a childish excuse, I knew, but it had been all I could think of. I didn't have any family to kill off for the day, and I'd never learned to drive so I couldn't claim car problems or an accident.

They'd tried to get me to let them come to me, with a notary, but that had led to another lie: *I'm constantly in the bathroom, no you can't come over.* That had been embarrassing, but there'd been little I could do about it. Oh well, I still had a sizeable nest egg in my bank account, so I didn't need to work right away. Even at New York City prices.

I stared out at the street below, always busy with cars and people walking by. The buildings across from me were all brownstone apartments and residential areas. Down the street there was a shop on the corner, I could just pop out and buy whatever I needed and come back home in a matter of minutes. I didn't have to drive to a store to pick things up.

I could take the bus wherever I wanted to go, even to another state, so I had a freedom here that I didn't have in more rural areas. I loved that, and had been delighted with it at first, but as the days passed, reality set in. I didn't have anywhere to go, there was nobody I could pop over to see. I was alone here, and even the lure of countless museums and interesting sites couldn't draw me out of the apartment.

I wanted to go back to Nashville. In my head and heart, that place had become home. I went to the couch that had filled me with glee when I first saw it, but now only left me with a sore ass because it was so hard, and picked up my notebook. I'd filled it with new songs and would soon need another one.

Some were only sketches, outlines of the song that might never be. Others were finished with music to go with it. Those would go on the album I had planned. If I ever signed that contract. The producer the agent had introduced me to was a bitch. She'd looked me up and down, snarled her nose a little, and had looked at the agent.

"Seriously?" she'd asked the agent before she sighed. "Fine, we'll fit her in to the schedule somewhere. I hope you're right. There isn't much market for her style nowadays, but maybe she can make a comeback for it."

"Well, there's a reason "Man, I Feel Like a Woman" is still popular on karaoke lists. I have a feeling Ember has the next hit in her, I just know she does," the agent, a balding man named Pete, had replied.

I'd just stood there, numb, but with the knowledge that I was this close to a record contract. It wasn't with one of the powerhouse labels, but it was a label. Or so I'd thought at the time. Now, I knew this was all wrong. I needed to go out somewhere. I'd been cooped up in this place too long. All weekend, I realized as I went into the tiny, cold bathroom to do something with my hair.

I put it up in a bun and found a pair of jeans, a long cream colored sweater, and a pair of boots to wear underneath my coat. When I walked out of the apartment, my skin was clear of any makeup, but I didn't care. I was supposed to be sick, right?

I knew it wasn't likely I'd see anyone who knew I was supposed to have signed a contract today, so I went down to the bus stop without a worry. The sun was starting to go down, so some of the places I could visit would be closed, but not many. It was New York City, another place that barely slept.

I headed to an art museum that was known around the

world, and wandered around there for a couple hours. Then I went to another museum about World War II, and that brought the world down around me. I was somber by the time I left the museum and just walked out of the place with no destination in mind. I had nowhere to be and no one to see; well, not now that my appointment time had passed me by.

I saw a diner down one street, one of those old-fashioned aluminum deals where the windows were all steamy, and decided some artery-clogging goodness was just what I needed right now. I went in and sat down at an empty booth, and smiled when a gum-popping waitress came up to the table with a grin.

"What'll it be, sugar?" she asked with a wink, and I looked down at her nametag.

"I'll have a cheesesteak platter please, Pam," I said with a wink of my own. The menu was on a large board overhead of the cooks behind the counter, and I'd picked out what my stomach had growled over the most.

"Coming up. Oh, what do you want to drink?" she managed to ask all of that while she still popped her gum, and I liked her spunk. She was definitely a character.

"Just some tea please." I forgot I was in the north though, not the south.

"Hot, cold, herbal or regular, sweetened or unsweetened?" She kind of rolled her eyes a little but softened it with a smirk.

"Sweet and cold please. I didn't get this figure by watching calories, now did I?" She'd inspired me, and when she heard my response she laughed.

We were good then. I liked her direct, bold style, and knew she could be a friend. If I stayed in New York.

Another sigh and I tapped my fingers against the table. A new song in my head, already. It could be like that, you know? One day, you couldn't write a song if your life depended on it, and the next? You just couldn't stop writing.

I pulled out a napkin, fished around in my coat pocket until I found a pen, I always kept a pen in my coat pocket, and started to write. I had filled up two napkins by the time she came back with my drink and dinner.

"What are you writing, sweet cheeks?" She slid the plate in front of me gently and put the glass down behind the plate.

"Just a song." I didn't want to go into much more than that, but she got this amazed look in her eyes.

"I do know you! It's been bugging me since you walked in, but I couldn't place where I knew you from. You're that singer on YouTube! Ember! Oh my god, girl! I hope you're up here doing an album because you need to be!"

I stared at her, my own mouth hung open, as she talked. She knew me? From my videos online? How?

"I'm, well, I'm supposed to start one, but…"

"But what? Girl, you can't let a voice like that go unheard!" She stared at me, her eyes taking inventory. "Is it a man?"

"Probably. Yes." I felt awkward, but she seemed like she was the kind who gave good advice.

Pam looked around the diner, it was mostly empty, and then sat down across from me. "If a man is worth it, you should do what it takes to make it work. I'm thirty-nine-years-old, and this is what my life will be. I chose the wrong guy, the wrong path, but I didn't have the talent you have. You have to find a way to make both work."

"I could do that, if I went back to Nashville." I picked at my sandwich, my thoughts a whirl in my head.

"Would that be a bad thing?"

"I left. I made a choice, based on information I thought was good. Now, I'm not so sure." I plucked at a string of cheese and took a bite of it while she thought.

"I'm not going to pry, but it sounds to me like you need to work things out before you can move forward. And, baby girl, with that voice? You're going to move forward fast. You just have to sort out what's behind you. And he'd better be worth it. You've got a fan for life now." She patted my hand and stood up. "But let me stop butting in. Eat your meal. You need your strength."

She moved away, and I smiled as she went to another customer who had just walked in. What a sweet woman. With some really good advice to give too. I'd known it since the moment I left. Running away had not been a good idea. It had been a very stupid idea, in fact.

I had been so caught up in protecting my heart, I'd done the one thing I was afraid of someone else doing. I'd broken it, all by myself. I hadn't needed help.

Kevin hadn't deserved the way I'd treated him. The man had proven he cared about me and what happened to me, time after time. Not just with money or sex, but in the way he thought about me, the way he always protected me, and the way he held me. Men who didn't care couldn't hold a woman like that, surely?

I knew he must have loved me, he had to love me.

I finished my sandwich and ordered a piece of chocolate pie for dessert. A glass of wine came with the pie, and I grinned. Only in New York would you get wine at a diner. Pam gave me another smirk as I sipped at the cold, pink liquid. Not muscadine, but whatever.

I tried to decide what to do. Go back and surprise him? Would he even speak to me? God, I hadn't thought about that. Maybe he was so angry that I'd left like that he wouldn't want to see me? Maybe he wouldn't welcome me back with open arms.

Damn. What should I do? I could try to text him, but that didn't seem appropriate either. Call him? I ate the pie while I thought about it.

I had signed a lease on the apartment, but maybe I could get out of it since I'd only been there for a week? I wondered if there was a clause about that somewhere, one that said I had time to change my mind. I had a feeling there wasn't. Housing was expensive, and empty rentals didn't stay empty long in the city that so many dreamed about calling home. I'd barely found the loft apartment at all; my agent's cousin owned the place or I would've still been looking.

Maybe I should keep it though? Just in case Kevin didn't want me and I had to come back? Or, if he did, it was still somewhere to sleep when I was in this part of the world.

I wasn't sure.

I knew I'd lived my life on the fringes, and I'd always

left choices up to those I'd deemed adults. Even when I was stealing money from my mom for food when I was a kid, I'd waited until I knew for certain she wasn't going to go out and buy any. She might change her mind, through the haze of drugs, and try to take care of me.

Then, I'd been little more than a doormat for Graham. He'd made the choices because he was the man, and he was the one in charge. I hadn't protested, at least not until the end. I'd decided to let others choose for me. And Kevin had done a lot of that too. I'd let him choose so much for me because I was afraid of my choice.

Well, now it was time to make a choice for myself. I'd decided to come to New York, and that had been a stupid idea, but now I could make it all better. I could make a choice that was right.

I picked up my phone, got rid of the dozen notifications that were on my home screen, and filed through my contacts until I found Kevin's number. I selected his name and hit call. I waited, my nerves strung tight and my foot tapping against the floor. I'd die before he picked up, I just knew I would.

18

KEVIN

Kevin

"What do you mean, you can't find her?" I growled into the phone and clenched my fist. I could feel a knot form in my jaw as anger poured into my veins. Why couldn't people find one woman in New York? It wasn't like people were hard to track now; everybody had cell phones, right?

I wanted to shout at Emily, but it wasn't her fault. She wasn't the kind to break the law and try to track someone with their phone. I knew what she'd say if I shouted at her, anyway. It was the same thing my brain kept shouting at me.

Why don't you try to call her?

Because I was afraid she wouldn't answer. If Veronica

had scared her off, she probably didn't want to talk to me anyway. My heart clutched at the thought that I wouldn't see her again, but I told myself to calm down. We'd find her. One way or another.

Sooner rather than later, I hoped.

I'd ended the call with Emily soon after that and went into the bathroom to shower. That dream, damn, it was still on my mind. The way she'd been out of reach, right there one second, and then gone, until I'd found her. I wanted that sweet bliss of reunion with Ember.

I could have sex with any woman, or even have a nice long wank, but that wasn't what I wanted. I didn't want relief. I wanted Ember. She was the only relief that would soothe me.

I slumped against the shower wall and wondered if I was on the verge of losing my mind. Nothing else mattered, only Ember. I didn't care about deals in London, or that one of our hotels was an embarrassment. That could all wait until after I'd found Ember and satisfied myself that she wouldn't leave me again.

She'd been afraid from the start, and who could blame her? I'd thrown a world at her that she'd never lived in, never dreamed of, and hadn't made a single promise to her, other than the fact that I'd make her a star. I'd have a long talk with the managers at the bar when things calmed down. They should have gone over the contract with her before she'd had time to see Veronica.

Although, I knew I couldn't blame them. It had been at my feet to take care of Ember. I'd promised myself that, and I'd failed. The water remained hot, but it didn't soothe me.

I washed myself and my hair then got out of the shower. With a towel around my hips, I dried off, shaved, and pulled clothes out of the bag I'd brought with me. A pair of navy blue slacks, a light blue button-up shirt, and a jacket to match the slacks. I'd just thrown things in the bag. I hadn't really planned, and my hands had chosen my normal business attire.

By the time I dressed my hair was dry, and I looked in the mirror to see a handsome face, a powerful body, and the mark of confidence that money lent to any suit. It didn't matter how much the suit cost, or how good the tailor was when it came to my eyes, though. Sadness lived there now, and I couldn't seem to shake it.

I gave a scowl and walked away. I didn't know what I'd do, but I couldn't sit in this room and wait. I found myself outside, a car waiting for me. I told the driver to take me to the center of the city, and then asked him to let me out. I wandered the streets until I found a café.

I watched for signs of Ember. Every person who passed could have been her, and I scanned the crowds until my head swam. I ordered a coffee and a donut. I didn't taste either, but the coffee helped to warm me up. I didn't bother to make small talk with the waitress. I just ordered and looked away, too busy scanning the crowds to notice her.

I went out into the streets and knew this would be impossible. There were too many people and too many places she could be. I kept walking though, the Italian leather of my shoes soft, but little protection from the cold. For a while, I stopped at another café, a place where I could see more people as they walked by.

I didn't want to let defeat in, and I refused to think about the negatives for long. I would find her, I just knew I would. I passed shops full of expensive, luxury goods, buildings where millions of dollars could be made or lost in an instant, and saw a thousand women who paled in comparison to Ember, but could obviously afford only the best in life.

I decided then I was in the wrong part of the city. Ember wouldn't be here. She'd go where the apartments were a more reasonably priced, even if those prices still outpaced those we'd found in Nashville. I had to go to that part of the city then.

I found a car rental place and soon left the lot with a car made for city driving. Luxurious city driving. I headed toward the outskirts of the city, to the places where people took the buses more often because cars were too much of an expense. I'd wasted the morning, I knew that as soon as I found my way in a less affluent borough. This was more like Ember. This was where she'd gravitate to.

Not because she'd grown up poor, but because she didn't have much use for shiny and pretty. She liked practical and pretty. I grinned at that, she was definitely frugal, but she did like to have pretty things every now and then.

I parked the car and paid for parking before I looked around. I found a café off to my right and went there. A good spot to sit and watch for one curly-headed blonde woman to pass me by. That was something else about, Ember.

When all the other women were spending a fortune on making their hair straight, she embraced her curls. I preferred them to the straight version that she would sometimes wear. It took her hours to iron out all of those curls, so I could see why she rarely did it.

I knew I was just killing time, but I couldn't sit still in that room. It would have driven me crazy. I hadn't counted on the cold, or the snow that soon began to drop, so I left the café and found a shop that sold coats. I bought one that wasn't my normal quality but would keep the cold out. I zipped up the two black wool panels, added a scarf before I paid, and left the store.

Now. Which way should I go?

The sun had started to set by now, and I knew it would only get harder to see her. Maybe I should go back to the hotel. I chose a direction without even thinking about it and walked. I walked until I couldn't even remember where the car was, but found myself in a quaint little street with a lot of brownstones and trees.

I passed a lot of people, but none of them were Ember. I saw a diner up ahead, shiny and well-lit. The steam on the windows screamed warmth at me, otherwise I'd have ignored it. But it was the exact kind of place where I'd find Ember.

I walked up to the place and saw a tall redheaded woman serving coffee to a man. A little further down, still with her scarf wrapped around her throat, I could see her.

At last. Ember. I stood still in front of the window where she was sat and couldn't believe it. I'd found her!

I placed my hand on the glass and she looked up, startled. She looked at the hand and then past it to look into my eyes. I saw her brown eyes go wide before she stood up and ran out of the diner.

"Kevin!" She launched herself into my arms, and I pulled her in tight, determined to never let her go.

"Ember. Oh my god, I found you!" I kissed every inch of her face as I held her in my arms against my chest. Then I sank down onto my knee and pulled the box from my pocket. "I can't believe I found you, but now that I have, please, Ember, will you marry me? Never leave me again and be my wife?"

I opened the box and heard cheers behind us. I saw all the people that had been in the diner, plus a few people that had been about to walk by were all now an audience for my proposal.

"Ember?" I prodded, an eyebrow lifted.

"What?" she asked, her eyes only on the ring in the box.

"Will you marry me?" I felt a tight knot in my stomach grow when she looked into my eyes, hers filled with tears.

I felt that knot grow even more when she put her hands over her mouth and sobbed. Her eyes were on the rock in that box. A small diamond surrounded by an intricate gold lace that would suit her finger perfectly. Small, tasteful, just like Ember.

"Ember? Please?" I whispered as a knot had formed in my throat that I couldn't speak around.

She sank down to her knees, onto cold pavement, and

placed her right hand over my cheek. "I would love to be your wife, Kevin. Yes, I'll marry you."

The crowd, now a little bigger, went wild and I didn't care. I pulled her back to me and kissed her with all the relief I felt inside.

When we finally stood up I didn't want to take my eyes off of her, but there was a woman, a waitress if the apron around her waist was any indication, came up to Ember and hugged her.

"That him?" I heard her ask and wondered who she was to Ember.

"That's him. Oh, that's him." Ember grinned and introduced us.

"Hi, Pam, great to meet you."

"You too, Kevin. You have a special lady there. Take care of her from now on. And get her back to Tennessee; it's too cold for her up here in the frozen north!" We all laughed at the last part, then we were sent on our way.

Ember gathered her bag, paid her bill, and we left the sidewalk where I'd proposed with a shiny new diamond on Ember's finger. I couldn't believe I'd found her, and I wondered if I was still asleep. I knew I wasn't, but I had to wonder.

"I can't believe I found you," I said as we walked hand in hand in the direction of her apartment. She hadn't done bad, if she'd already found an apartment and had herself set up.

"You know me too well, I guess." She smiled up at me, and I kissed her on top of the head.

We went into the warm building, up the elevator, and

she walked me into her apartment. It was clean, minimalist, and didn't suit her at all. It was nice, for New York, but it wasn't her kind of place. It was too cramped, with nowhere for her to hide.

"So can you tell me what happened?" I asked once we were on the couch, hot coffee on the table in reach. She sat down beside me, her feet tucked under her with her arm on the back of the couch.

"I got spooked, I guess." Honest and direct, that was my Ember.

"What spooked you?" I knew, but I wanted her side of the story.

"This woman showed up, this beautiful, gorgeous woman who looked like she knew exactly which moisturizer to use at night and which to use in the morning. She had a picture of a kid. She said you'd talked her into a threesome and had then left her. Denied the baby was yours."

"I did. I stood right in a courtroom and denied it," I told her as I swept a lock of hair behind her ear.

"You did? How could you, Kevin? Fuck, that's just, that's so wrong." She'd jumped up off the couch by then and had started to pace. "You should at least support him."

"But he's not mine, Ember. I've never met the woman. She's got a mental illness and a fixation on me. I went to school with her brother years ago, and well, she's not very healthy. I'm not sure how she ended up in Tennessee, but I'm sorry about that. None of what she said was true. I'd never do anything like that. If I had a child, I'd take care of it and be part of its life. I wouldn't abandon it like that."

She paused, looked uncertain, then came back to sit with me.

"Really? She's crazy?" She sighed and looked sad. "I knew there was something wrong with her when she came in; she frightened me, but then she calmed down."

"She's on a lot of medication, Ember. We can't really be angry with her, but last year I told my side of the story. She's not supposed to come anywhere near me. I guess the restraining order from England doesn't work here, but if you want me to, I'll get another one for here. Somehow." I wasn't sure how that would work, but I'd get our legal team on it, just in case.

"I guess that's all then. I should have waited, but, well, you know me? If there's a stupid choice and right choice, I always go for stupid."

"No, Ember. You choose with your heart, not your head. That's nothing to be ashamed of." I took her hand and pulled her close. My body screamed at me to get her naked and to taste every inch of her flesh, but my mind said to take it slow. It wanted to just be with her and enjoy the feel of her warm and solid against me.

My phone buzzed, and I moved to pull it out of my coat pocket. I had to reach across the back of the couch to get the phone, so it stopped ringing by the time I'd pulled it out and opened the case. There was another missed call on the display.

"You called me?" I asked, not sure how I'd missed the call. I should have felt it vibrate, but maybe I'd been distracted.

"Yeah, I wanted to find out if I could come back. I hated

myself for how I'd left it and decided that I'd made a mistake."

"It's alright now, Ember. We don't ever have to be apart again, not like that anyway." I pulled her into me and knew peace at last.

19

EMBER

Ember

I pulled away from the only man I ever really loved and waited for him to decide what we were going to do next. He inhaled sharply, and his eyes burned into mine, our eyes a twinkle in the darkness. I hadn't turned on many lights, just the small one over the stove in the kitchen, and the room was mostly dark.

I'd thought he'd turn me away when I called; instead, he'd shown up out of thin air. So close I could touch him, and then he'd proposed. I'd wanted to scream with joy, but I'd thrown myself into his arms while my face reached for his. He'd been cold, almost frozen, and as soon as we made it into my apartment, I'd made coffee to warm him up. We'd barely touched, but his hand was warm when it brushed against my cheek.

Now, I wanted so much more from him. I wanted his kiss again, I wanted his touch.

He leaned into me and kissed me, as if he'd read my mind. His fingers brushed against my cheek before they dove into my hair to tilt my head back. His tongue slicked into my mouth and teased mine into play.

I couldn't stop the shiver that went down my spine as his tongue stroked over mine, our mouths fused together in a way that made it hard to breathe. I didn't care, I moaned into his mouth as my desire flooded into my veins, and he deepened our kiss.

I felt loved for the first time in my life. This was real romantic love that filled my heart and made it swell until I thought I would explode into a thousand pieces. I loved Kevin, maybe even more than I'd loved my grandmother. I'd found what I hadn't known I was missing, and now it was mine forever.

I wrapped myself around Kevin, and he pulled me up. This allowed me to wrap my legs around his waist as I was pulled higher up his body. Ah, he wanted to carry me, I figured out as he stood up with me safe against his chest. My arms wound around his neck, and I clung tighter to him as he began to move toward the bed.

Kevin let me go for a moment, his respiration fast and labored as we fell in a tangle of limbs to the bed. His hips pressed into mine from above, the pressure in just the right places as he looked down at me, his elbows locked to keep him in place above me.

"Are you mine?" he asked me, his eyes glued to mine as I suddenly stopped to watch him.

How could he doubt it? I'd said yes, but still, he worried. I knew that was my fault and took his face into my hands and looked right into those beautiful eyes of his.

"Every day for the rest of your life, I'm yours, Kevin! For as long as you want me, I'm yours. If that's forever, then that's what I'll take." I let my brown eyes meet his, the intensity of his gaze and my words made my heart race as he stared back at me. How long did he want me for?

"Forever, Ember? You'll be mine forever?" he asked, the words hesitant, as though he'd never spoken them before. I doubted he'd ever planned to say them before he met me.

"Forever, Kevin. No holds barred, no more doubts, always yours and only yours."

"Ember, I should tell you…" but I didn't let him finish. What else was there to say?

"Not now, later, baby. All I want you to do right now is fuck me, Kevin, please. I've missed you so desperately, and I want you to take me to the place only you can take me to." I held a finger to his lips but pulled it away when he moved to whisper into my ear.

"My dick has missed you more." He pulled at the clothes that kept me warm and then threw some of his own away.

His fingers slid down to the part that had missed his touch the most and felt the simultaneous sensation of an ache that had been soothed while at the same time, a new ache increased. I danced against him, my body more than ready for his touch.

"My heart has missed you even more than that." The words came out halting, but I heard them and looked up at him.

I couldn't breathe, my body stilled, and hope flared as he waited for an answer.

"My heart missed you too, Kevin." I stroked his cheek with eager fingers, and his head turned to kiss the digit.

He leaned down to kiss me tenderly, his tongue a soft stroke against mine until it began to mimic the movement of his fingers, and tender thoughts took flight. I wanted relief.

"I love you." I breathed the words at last, almost too low to hear but he heard them.

"I lo…" His voice cut out and a growl came out as he pulled away.

I thought he was going to do something else, to maybe say we shouldn't do this for some stupid reason, but he was only taking off the rest of his clothes. It was only a second before he was back between my thighs, his lips right beside my ear.

"I'm sorry, Ember, I can't wait, baby. I've missed all of this too much. I've missed you too much." He pulled me tight to his hips then, and I looked up at him where he rested on his knees. He wasn't finished with words yet, though. "I love you, Ember, as I've never loved anyone ever before in my life. I just want you to know that."

With those words he sank into me, every last thick inch of him, until I thought there was no room left. He filled me as he opened me, and every inch of him stroked me as he pulled away, only to dive in deeper, going further than he had before. I clutched at his shoulder as he sank into me over and over, and the world narrowed down to this one place in this one moment.

"Fuck," I gasped into his shoulder as I held him tight to me, and my teeth sank into his flesh as he began to go even deeper, harder.

"Fuck, it's so good. So fucking good, Ember!" Kevin groaned the words out, a sound of almost pain, but it was actually intense pleasure. He was as close as I was to the edge.

My thoughts stopped when his fingers found my clit, combined with the sensation of my nipples rubbing into his chest while his cock pounded until it all fused into a storm of sensation that left me floating, barely able to breathe.

"I want you, Kevin, forever."

"Forever, Ember, forever is what you'll get." He moaned his response, his hips a steady thrust against me that matched in time with his words.

We moved together, our hips joined, our mouths fused, with love the glue that held us together.

I loved him, more than anything else in my life. I knew I loved him because I felt it, and as I exploded around his cock, I was love. His love.

Kevin followed me into the dark zone where our cries blended as my smooth thighs cradled his body gently.

We clung together as we caught our breath, our bodies still not done. I wanted more, and the hardness of him inside me told me he wasn't quite done yet either.

He held me close, his head in my neck as he tried to catch his breath. We slept tangled together. I woke up when he dragged me into the shower with a carefree laugh. I wanted to grouse that I needed more sleep, but

Kevin only washed me gently and ignored my protests. He took me back to the bed, pulled me close and whispered into my ear, "I want in that pussy of yours again, Ember. Will you let me in?" He punctuated it with a kiss just behind my earlobe, and I'd have agreed to anything at that point.

He surprised me when he moved down between my thighs. What else was he going to get inside of me then? I soon found out when he parted my thighs, and his tongue found my opening before he dived deep to lick up my juices.

His fingers followed his tongue, and his pressed them into me, two and then three.

"You're so tight, Ember. Is that too much?" He was always careful with me. And he'd asked me stupid questions at the wrong time.

Like when I couldn't speak because he was blowing my mind!

"It's fine. Fine, Kevin." I could only pant the words out, too caught up in the sensations he was making me feel to be coherent.

"Fine? Hmm. I'm not sure that's acceptable. I want good, Ember, it feels good." His words were rough but hot, so hot I could feel myself clench around the fingers he now thrust into me.

"That's good, fuck, that's good, Kevin. I swear, don't stop, please don't stop." I gripped the cover beneath me and strove to find that edge as he teased me for a while longer.

"Oh that's much better, Ember. And how about now?" He paused to blow on my clitoris, and I knew that was just his way of teasing me more. He'd get his tongue on me soon enough, but would it be before I died or after?

I could feel sparks deep inside of me, each time his fingers plunged into me, and I knew I'd be finished before he was, long before.

"Later I'm going to get my hands on those gorgeous nipples of yours, but for now, I think you want my attention... *here.*"

He said the word here quietly, then his lips closed around my clit. The liquid heat of his mouth was too much of a sweet torment to fight, and I moaned his name. His tongue flicked at the swollen bud as I twisted beneath him, my body alive as the pleasure he gave me spread through every square inch of me. He was going to kill me with that tongue, I just knew it.

Over and over I felt the waves pass through me, and I felt his tongue, a slick pleasure that sent me further and further. I was almost beyond the point where it was comfortable, but Kevin continued to tease my tortured clit as he placed a palm over my lower abdomen to hold me down. He ignored my weak protests until it started all over again, and I couldn't move. I was too relaxed to do anything else.

I couldn't believe I could feel it again so soon, but he drove through that odd feeling to send me even higher.

Kevin thrust his fingers into my liquid walls as I floated in heaven, the spastic clench of my muscles sucked his fingers in deep as he sent me higher with my ankles dug into the bed. But he let up at last, and I came back to earth slowly, aware of the deep throb of his cock against me as he held me close. We were both hot, sweaty, but I didn't care. I held him to me as he touched me everywhere he dared to at the moment.

"Turn over," he finally whispered when my breathing was calm, and I wasn't so hot anymore.

I moved to my knees and waited for him to decide what to do next. His hand cupped my ass, and I patiently let him explore me. I could feel how hot and swollen my body was, and I knew he'd slide into me easily.

He proved me right when I felt him give a slight nudge of his hips and he slid into me. My body was hungry for every inch of him, and I felt the way he opened me with delight.

He began to move, his cock too eager to wait as I squeezed around him.

I felt him moving and felt the pleasure of it as my body made room for him.

What had felt like too much was now a new sensation, a good one that made me want even more.

He drove into me, his hands tight on my hips, and I kept myself upright despite the growing strength of each thrust. His hands moved to the bottom of my back and pushed down. "Your back is beautiful in the moonlight, Ember. Let me look at you."

I sank my head down to the mattress and didn't care if it made my skin shine in the moonlight. He wanted to look at me, then he could look his fill. He'd told me once that my spine was one of the most beautiful parts about me. Perfect, womanly, seductive. I didn't know that was a thing, but if it brought out the poet in Kevin, so be it.

With a sharp cry and a tight grip of his fingers, Kevin let go and I sighed, completely happy. He came down beside me and smiled a sleepy smile.

"You thirsty?" he asked, and I nodded. "I'll get something then."

He came back with two bottles of mineral water, and we both drank them almost empty. "When do you want to get married?"

"I don't know." I could only blink at him. "Shouldn't we wait a little while?"

"I'm not going to force you into anything, but I'd do it tonight if we had someone to sign the papers." He laughed, and I grinned.

"Well, I've not done much properly in my life, so I guess I shouldn't start now. But I would like a proper wedding, with a dress and flowers. You know, all of that kind of stuff."

"I think I can wait a few months. You're right, you should have what you want. I get you in the end, so it doesn't matter to me. So long as you're happy, Ember."

"I want you happy too," I protested and leaned over to look in his eyes. "It's not just about me, you know? You have to be happy too."

"I've got you, and one day, your last name will be Thompson. I'm more than happy, Ember. I'm complete. I didn't know how fractured I was until you came along. But you made me whole, baby. I don't need anything else."

Let's just say I could have done an *aw* for the entire world.

20

EMBER

Ember

Three Months Later

I put the cap on my lip gloss and looked in the mirror. Not bad. I probably should have made more of an effort to put on makeup, but it was our wedding day. I didn't want to look like something I would never be in the pictures.

I'd had a makeup artist do my makeup the day before, to show me what they planned to do, and I'd sent them home. I didn't like it. Oh, I looked good enough, beautiful even, but it wasn't the woman Kevin proposed to that stared back. It was the singer on stage look, as I thought of it. Not me.

We'd been through some rough times since I'd gone

back to Nashville. Graham had popped up and tried to make me pay him back for my plane ticket to England. When I got done explaining my side of the story to the DA, and told him about the drugs Graham had stashed in my guitar case, the matter soon dropped. He'd also wanted to claim authorship of a couple of my songs. I didn't think so, even if they were about what a douchebag he was; he had no part in writing them, they were all mine.

Kevin's legal team had handled it all well, and like I'd said, when I mentioned drugs, Graham soon shut up and pissed off back to Kentucky. He'd lost some teeth, lost weight, and his hair was long and dirty. I didn't miss him a bit, not even a little drop. He'd been a mistake from the word go, and now I was about to put him behind me.

"You alright?" Sarah asked as she came into the room. She looked beautiful in a deep red satin. It was still winter, almost Valentine's Day, so I'd chosen dark colors for the wedding. We were getting married on Kevin's father's estate, a giant pile of wood and marble that I still couldn't get used to. The place was in North Carolina, and Kevin had his private jet pick Sarah and I up to bring us here.

"I'm fine. Thanks. Thank you for this. You're my only real friend, you know?" I smiled a wobbly smile, and she glared.

"Stop that. I've met the other new Thompson brides, you know? I think you'll get along just fine with them."

"Yeah, Jessi and Laura are really nice. I don't know how they ended up with those brothers of Kevin's, but if either brother is like Kevin; well, I guess there's a side the rest of us don't see, isn't there?"

"There must be. That Trent guy terrifies me, you know?" Sarah adjusted a dark brown curl then turned back to me. "It's almost time. Let's get that dress on, shall we?"

We turned to the dress. It was ivory lace with a satin underlay. The arms were a softer lace, but they went all the way down to my fingertips in a point. It was almost an old-fashioned style, but it was updated by a skirt that wasn't too puffy. The train was long, ten feet, but it came free of the skirt, so I didn't mind it too much. The wedding pictures would be stunning.

I felt kind of silly, stood there in my underwear in front of Sarah, but she'd been a friend to me from the moment we'd met. I'd invited Pam down, but she'd had to work, but she did send us a nice present and a thank you. I'd gone back to the diner before we'd left New York and got her number. I had a job in line for her that would change the world for her and her children.

But that was all for after the wedding. Today, I was a bride, and I'd stop plotting out other people's lives if it killed me. Sarah had to stand on a chair to lift the dress over my head, and it fell down around all of my curves and lines without a wrinkle. The tailor had done her job perfectly. I smoothed the lace down and looked up at Sarah.

"It's perfect isn't it?" I asked, my gaze dewy again.

"It's amazing, Ember. Just like you." She wiped a tear away beneath my eye, and I saw her smile had a wobble to it. Emotions weren't just affecting me then. They had her too.

"Come on, before we turn into two sodden old maids,"

she finally said, and I rushed to find my shoes. A soft, white Italian leather confection of a shoe was the choice I'd made for my wedding day. Expensive as all get out, but Kevin hadn't cared.

Sarah applied the final touch when she pinned the ivory lace veil to my head, and we walked out of the room that had been set up as our station. Emily joined us with a smile and all of three of us headed toward the back garden. Flowers from the greenhouse adorned white lace as we walked out to a tunnel that led to an area with a small pond, a gazebo, and a dozen or so chairs. It was mainly Kevin's family, but I didn't mind. They would be my family soon enough.

For a moment, the little girl in me wished my parents were here too, but I knew I was better off alone. They'd have raided the bathrooms looking for pills in medicine cabinets, and probably would have stolen the silver to sell off for more drugs. No, I was much better off.

My head came up a little more, and I walked down the aisle alone. That didn't bother me either. I was a strong, independent woman, except for when it came to Kevin. I needed him like spring flowers need the rain. He was my life and all I wanted.

After our honeymoon, I would start on my album, and in the spring, I'd go on tour. Just to the hotel bars for now, but in the summer, we were heading to Europe for music festivals. And yes, one of the stops was to visit London again. Kevin said I deserved a second go at England, and I had a feeling he was right.

"You look gorgeous, but you always do," Kevin said as I stepped up to him.

"I won't let you go, and I won't go on without you," I promised him. He'd told me about his dreams, the wedding, and how I'd slip away. It was one of the reasons we weren't marrying in a church, even though I'd been baptized as a Catholic. I'd never completed my training anyway, so it wasn't a big deal to me.

I liked being out in the open anyway. Kevin liked it too, and I smiled at him. He was gorgeous in a tuxedo, and with the sun going down behind us, we finally became husband and wife. The family made a lot of noise for us, and we all went into the main dining hall to enjoy a wedding supper fit for a king.

Kevin had been kind and had insisted we have a small wedding. He knew that was all we'd have anyway. I only had a couple of people to invite, so he'd insisted on family only. I saw one face I knew wasn't family, and knew that must be Henry, Kevin's best friend.

As I looked at him, I realized the man had stood behind Kevin during the wedding and felt embarrassed. I'd been so captivated by my fiancé I hadn't noticed the very handsome man behind him. The man should have been on magazine covers, and for all I knew he might have been. My eyebrow lifted as he tried to flirt with Emily, but she ignored him.

Was there romance there? I bit the inside of my lip and tried not to laugh. Emily, perfect, always poised, Emily, looked just a tad flustered at the other side of the table.

My attention was soon taken up by the reception, and

when Kevin stood up, a sheepish grin on his face that soon turned cocky, I knew he was about to do something.

"Hi there, folks. I've, uh, I've got a little song here I want to sing for my wife. She inspired me, and well, I know I can't do her talent justice, but this comes from the heart."

He picked up a guitar, and then, my husband began to sing a song about loneliness, a loneliness that his flame had taken away, and sometimes that flame was only an ember, but he carried it with him always. My heart melted, and I couldn't help it, I stood up and screamed with joy. Something I'd never have imagined doing so long ago, but now? Well, spontaneous was in my vocabulary now. I made a note to myself to get ahold of that song and develop it with him. It was a keeper, and his voice made something in me melt. The man had a singing career in front of him, if he ever gave up the hotel business. Maybe I could get him to do some backing tracks. I forgot to care for a little while as the song came to an end and my husband came to me and swept me up in his arms.

Before long, we were alone, in the perfect honeymoon spot for us. A cabin, deep in the woods of Asheville, North Carolina. Kevin drove us to the cabin we'd rented and got our bags out of the trunk as I opened the door. He dropped the bags as soon as I closed the door, and I turned to look at him quizzically.

"I've wanted to find out what you've had on underneath that dress for hours now, Ember." His heart was in his eyes, and mine responded with a tight squeeze that left me breathless.

"Just some lingerie, my dear. Your wife's knickers." I

teased him with the British word for underwear and saw his pulse increase in his neck.

I tried not to pounce on him, but it was hard. He had on a black t-shirt, and for the first time ever, I saw him in a pair of jeans. A black leather jacket kept the cold at bay, but we didn't need it now. I began to say something else, I didn't know what, because in a second, I was in his arms, my body wrapped around his as our lips came together.

We'd always burned hot like that, even when we knew we had hours alone to ourselves. I felt his lips on mine, our hands tangled as we pushed clothing away and then came together all over again. We broke away to look at each other with the glee of the newly married once more, and then I led him up the stairs I'd spotted. There had to be a bedroom up there somewhere. As soon as we found the room, we flicked on a light and headed for the bed. We didn't care about the fine accessories or how dim the lights were, although it was a romantic dim; we just wanted to be naked and wrapped around each other.

Our clothes disappeared, and then we were under the covers. I knelt over Kevin, our mouths fused together as I straddled his hips eagerly. I trembled with excitement, anticipation, and happiness. Even my legs shook as I kissed him with total abandon. I didn't allow thoughts to intrude. I simply licked at his lips. I roamed down and explored his neck and imprinted his taste on my mind all over again. I let my fingers skim over his pecs, delighted at the texture, the silky smoothness of his skin. My thighs readjusted to his hips, and I watched the way his eyes shot to mine. But I wasn't finished just yet.

My eyes drank him in, and my lips traced the place where his neck met his chest, the gentle curve of his ribs, down to that lush area where his waist dipped into his hips. I loved the smoothness of his skin, over every inch of him. I'd never liked hairy men and the fact that Kevin was mostly smooth delighted me.

Kevin decided he didn't want to be a bystander though. My body arched into his touch and chased the sensations of his fingers on me with eager delight. With strong hands he pushed me up so he could look at me in the moonlight.

"You're beautiful, Ember, so fucking beautiful." He sighed the words as he traced his fingers down every part of me, from my cheeks, across my lips, then over my chin and neck. He tortured me when he got to my breasts and teased both of my nipples.

I shivered when his fingers teased me into a mess of whimpers and tried to stop him. I wanted to explore him, I wanted to touch and taste him, but he was busy doing that to me. His fingers moved when I said his name, down to trace along my waist, over my tummy, and back to my ass. His hands wrapped around the firm globes of my buttocks and pulled me down to grind into his hips. That pushed my center into the ridge of his length between us. I lost my mind then.

I dug my hands into his shoulders and rode him like that. His hands guided me and we rocked together, our naked bodies on fire. We could have shifted just a fraction of an inch, and he'd have slid inside of me but the friction was beautiful, too beautiful to just give up.

"Kevin," I said as a warning. I was so close, so very close.

Did he want to be inside of me, because if he did, now was the time.

"Just let me watch you, Ember. Let me see you fly away," he answered, the words the first he'd spoken since we got into the house.

I did the only thing I could do, I complied. I'd give him whatever he wanted and give it gladly. I smiled down at him as our hips moved together, his face pale in the moonlight, and a mask of concentration as he watched me. That was the face that I loved, the face I wanted to wake up to each and every day. The face I would wake up to every day now that he was my husband. Later, I'd tell him about the baby that was on the way, the one that was so new, I wouldn't know if I didn't know my body so well. For now, I just wanted to enjoy him.

Kevin started to thrust his hips faster, to keep pace with my motions, and then I began to fly. My back arched, my breasts thrust out into the air, and I heard him sigh my name. He held my hips as I jarred to a halt, and the waves crashed over me. He watched me, watched the way my body shuddered over him, the way my hips moved of their own volition until they came to a complete stop. He watched as my head fell back, and I screamed a silent scream that was his name.

When it was done, Kevin pulled me down to his chest and held me until the shivers stopped. He cradled me to his chest to memorize the sound of his swiftly beating heart. He'd liked that. My fingers curled against his skin and felt the way his chest thudded with each beat. Strong and able, excited but steady.

Kevin made a sound, strangled need, before he moved with me in his arms. He pulled me under him as he expertly flipped me to turn us at the same time. Suddenly, I was on my back, with him between my thighs. I grinned and let my legs fall open to cradle him between my thighs, our tongues tangled together. He pulled away for a moment, his eyes steady on mine when he sank into me. I let him have his way and enjoyed the peaceful sensation we found when we were together like this. Kevin was bliss. Kevin in bed was that same bliss times ten. His green eyes caught my brown ones as he started to move; our bodies were attuned as we moved in time together.

He braced himself on his hands, and his head came down just as mine lifted so that our lips could fuse together. My legs wrapped around his waist, pulling him deeper into me. I could feel him within me, a sensation of having a million nerve endings touched at once.

I could hear the slick wetness of my pussy as he thrust into me, and I could smell our sweat combining on our heated bodies.

I ran my hands down his damp back, the silken feel of his skin delighting my fingertips.

I didn't care if I came now. I only wanted to feel Kevin, to see him and smell him, and most of all to taste him.

Our lips fused together once more, our tongues sliding together, over and around the other. Kevin moved with sweet determination, a pulse inside of me that scratched every itch of need I might have. Our breaths matched up, our hearts beat as one, and then we flew off into the sky together. He was my husband, and I was his wife. We were both now things we'd never thought we could be, but we were those things for each other.

"I love you, Ember," he rasped when he could form words again.

"I love you, Kevin." I was equally as breathless. "Shall we do that again?"

Kevin gave a soft laugh, and I smiled beside him in the darkness. We had a long time to do it all over again, and we would. Over and over again.

"In a moment, love. I'm trying not to die of happiness." His words stirred a warmth in my chest, and I turned to cuddle into his side. I was more than a little happy myself. Something I'd never thought I could be.

Kevin had decided to stop in that park that day, and he'd changed my life forever. I didn't know it at the time, but I'd changed his too. And now, we had each other. Forever.

DARK DESIRES
~ A billionaire dark romance series ~
Dark Desire
Dark Rules
Dark Secret
Dark Time
Dark Truth

BARRE TO BAR
~ A billionaire second chance series ~
Dancing With Lies
Dancing With Temptation
Dancing With Doubt
Dancing With Guilt
Dancing With Redemption

TWISTED INTENTION

~ A billionaire revenge romance series ~
Twisted Beauty
Twisted Love
Twisted Fate

Mafia's Obsession
~ A hot mafia romance series ~
Mafia's Dirty Secret
Mafia's Fake Bride
Mafia's Final Play

Screaming Demons
~ An MC romance series full of suspense ~
Rough Start
Rough Ride
Rough Choice
Rough Patch
Rough Return
Rough Road
Rough Trip
Rough Night
Rough Love

Standalone Contemporary Romance
Billionaire in Vegas
Billionaire Hunt
Billionaire's Game
Billionaire Retreat
Billionaire On Air

A Chance To Love
Somebody To Love
Not Mine To Love

Check out Summer's entire collection at
www.summercooper.com/books

ABOUT SUMMER COOPER

Thank you so much for reading. Without you, it wouldn't be possible for me to be a full-time author. I hope you enjoy reading my books as much as I do writing them.

Besides (obviously!) reading and writing, I also love cuddling my dogs, shouting at Alexa, being upside down (aka Yoga) and driving my family cray-cray!

Get in touch at
hello@summercooper.com
www.summercooper.com

facebook.com/summercooperauthor
instagram.com/summercooperauthor
goodreads.com/summercooper
bookbub.com/profile/summer-cooper